Praise for *Such a Pretty Girl*

"Wiess has created a spunky heroine—tough, darkly humorous, yet achingly vulnerable. . . . [A] gusty and effective thriller."

—*Kirkus Reviews* (starred review)

"*Such a Pretty Girl* is a riveting novel and fifteen-year-old Meredith is a wholly original creation: a funny, wise, vulnerable girl with the heart of a hero and the courage of a warrior. This gut-wrenching story will stay with you long after you finish the last page."

—Lisa Tucker, bestselling author of *The Song Reader*

"In clear, riveting prose, Laura Wiess boldly goes where other writers fear to tread. *Such a Pretty Girl* is gritty yet poetic, gut-churning yet uplifting—a compelling, one-of-a-kind read."

—A. M. Jenkins, author of *Damage* and *Out of Order*

"So suspenseful you'll wish you'd taken a speed-reading course. But slow down, because to rush would mean missing Laura Wiess's wonderfully precise language, her remarkable access to Meredith's darkest emotions, and a shocker of an ending—

—Tara Altebran

ness

such a pretty girl

laura wiess

POCKET BOOKS   MTV BOOKS

New York London Toronto Sydney

POCKET BOOKS, a division of Simon & Schuster, Inc.
1230 Avenue of the Americas, New York, NY 10020

ISBN-13: 978-1-4165-2183-9
ISBN-10:   1-4165-2183-6

This MTV Books/Pocket Books trade paperback edition January 2007

10   9   8

Manufactured in the United States of America

For information regarding special discounts for bulk purchases,
please contact Simon & Schuster Special Sales at
1-800-456-6798 or business@simonandschuster.com

To Chet,
who made a quiet wish
and
got way more
than he bargained for.

I'm so glad.

acknowledgments

I owe a debt of gratitude to my agent Barry Goldblatt, whose belief in this book brought us together, and whose drive, faith, and enthusiasm never faltered. Thank you for always giving me your straight-up opinion of my work. It means a lot.

Sincere thanks to my intrepid editor Jennifer Heddle for her keen insight, generous guidance, and skillful handling of such an intense issue. I'd also like to thank Jacob Hoye from MTV, Lauren McKenna, Lisa Litwack, and everyone at MTV/Pocket Books who worked to make this book happen. It's been a real pleasure.

Thanks to Cathy Atkins, Amy Butler Greenfield, Kristina Cliff-Evans, Lisa Firke, Shirley Harazin, Lisa Harkrader, Amanda Jenkins, Denise Johns, Cynthia Lord, Amy McAuley, Mary Pearson, Marlene Perez, Nancy Werlin, and Melissa Wyatt of the YACraft list for their 24/7 patience, humor, and wisdom. You're the best.

A deep curtsy to Paul Pinaha for his experimental upshot, Lauren Magda for her magical talent, and Emma Wiess for her wonderful, warm welcomes.

I'm grateful to Sgt. Cliff Kumpf of the Milltown PD for his expert assistance regarding law enforcement procedures, and to Warren Barrett for his technical advice. You guys were great, and any liberties taken after the fact are on me.

Loving thanks to my parents Bill and Barbara Battyanyi, for their endless support, encouragement, and for never being too busy to listen, no matter how odd the topic. Thank you, Sue, my sister and best friend, for reading my work and calling me in fits, offering to adopt my main character, Meredith, and give her a stable, loving home. You mean the world to me. Thanks also to my brother, Scott, for the laughter and the blackberries, always so dear to my heart. Special thanks to Bonnie Verrico and Sheila Schuler, for more than twenty-five years of outstanding friendship.

Most of all, love and thanks to my husband Chester, who willingly shouldered more than his fair share to give me time. Without his strength, generosity, and good heart, this book would not have been possible.

chapter one

They promised me nine years of safety but only gave me three.

Today my time has run out.

I sit on the curb at the back of the parking lot near the Dumpster. The waste from the condo complex bakes in this cumbersome green kiln and the stench is shocking, heavy with rancid grease and sickly-sweet decay. The association's tried to beautify the Dumpster, painting the rusty sides a perky green and relettering the faded RESIDENTS' USE ONLY sign, but the battered lid thwarts them, as it's warped from rough use and no longer seals the stewing fumes neatly in the box.

"Perfect," I mutter and take a drag off my cigarette. Blow a couple of smoke rings and tempt the crusading, condo cowboys to rush from their air-conditioned dens and snatch the forbidden smudge stick away.

But they won't. They keep their distance now, afraid my taint will rub off.

These adults who ache to interfere—convinced their quality-of-life ordinances and PC patrolling make them a village-raising-a-child—are the same people who picketed and wrote scathing letters to the editor to prevent my mother from renting a second condo in the front of the complex for my father's homecoming.

It didn't work, of course. My mother's attorney protected my father's rights and threatened to sue the complex owner if housing was denied. The owner caved, the condo was rented, and the neighbors were left reeling, hobbled by their own laws.

"I wish I could have found him a unit closer to ours, but this'll have to do for now," my mother had said earlier, spraying CK's Obsession along her neck and thighs. "And besides, it's only temporary until we can live like a family again." Her cheeks were pink, her voice breathy with anticipation. "He's really looking forward to it, Meredith. Being home with us, I mean. It's what's kept him going. I hope you can appreciate that."

I watched her and said nothing. Silence was the key to self-preservation.

"Now, where did I leave my . . . oh, there it is." She crossed to the bed, slipped off her robe, and smoothed the lace trim on her white La Perla panties. The matching bra was for show only, as she was almost flat on top. "And as far as this whole adjustment period thing goes . . . personally, I

2

would have let you spend the weekend at your grand-mother's like we'd planned so your father and I could have had a little time alone first, but that's not what he wanted." Frowning, she examined the delicate, rhinestone heart stitched onto the front of the panties. "Hmm. This better not make a bump under my dress. He wants us both here for him and I think that says a lot about forgiveness and a fresh start. We've *all* sacrificed, Meredith. I hope you un-derstand that, too."

I studied my thumb. Bit off a hangnail. Dead skin, so no pain. Not bad.

"Just stay *down*, will you?" She poked at the glittery heart, not seeming to notice my lack of response. "Oh, for . . . I don't have time for this. If it sticks up, I'll just have to cut it off." Impatient, she slid into her dress and pre-sented me with her back so I could zip the new red mini. It was a size two from a Lord & Taylor window display she'd designed at the mall and probably not intended for a thirty-nine-year-old with a stranglehold on her fading youth. "Careful. This is silk."

I eased up the zipper and lingered, one knuckle brushing the warmth of her neck.

"Time, Meredith." She pulled away and shook her hair, poked her feet into scarlet mules, and smoothed the dress from hipbone to hipbone. "No lumps, no bumps. Perfect."

3

I wandered over to her bureau and recapped the cologne as my mother continued her nervous chatter.

"I used this same shade of red in the WELCOME HOME! banner, the flowers in the living room, and the new guest towels, you know. In decorating, you want to tie everything together to create the impression of continuous harmony. I put touches of color in your father's condo, too. I think he'll be pleased. Oh, and I took three steaks out to thaw so now is not the time to go into that silly vegetarian kick." She glanced my way and shook her head. "And please, put on something decent before we get back. This is a celebration, not a wake. No overalls and *no more gray*. I mean it. Try to look cheerful for a change." She skimmed on lipstick and glanced at her watch. "Time to run. Tonight's going to be wonderful!"

Wrong, I'd wanted to say as she swept out in a blur of red silk. Tonight is when the obscene becomes the acceptable.

My father has been gone for three years. Long enough for the town to finally stop shunning us and for his victims to get counseling. Long enough for me to lose one social worker to pregnancy and two more hollow-eyed, twitchy ones to career burnout. Long enough for my mother to have been granted a divorce, had she ever applied for one. But she hasn't. Nor has she ever stopped visiting him in the Big House.

Today will be her final pilgrimage, and thanks to Megan's Law, everyone in town knows it.

My father's release date was given to all the local cops, school administrators, and youth group leaders. They got handouts with his name, photo, physical description, the crimes for which he was convicted, his home address, and license plate. The law says they aren't allowed to share the info with anyone else, but of course they did—who wouldn't?—so now we're marked for life. His picture is even posted on the New Jersey Sex Offender Internet Registry.

My mother ignores it all; the hostile undercurrents, the whispers and disparaging looks, the grim disgust in my grandmother's face, and the dogged blankness in mine.

Sharon Shale, my mother, does not see what she doesn't want to see.

She never has.

And for the last three years, she hasn't wanted to see *me*. At least not in private, when no one else is watching. She's always half-turned away, ahead of or behind me, tossing out words without watching to gauge their effect, cluttering my wake with complaints of attitude, dirty dishes, or stray eyebrows plucked into the sink. She acts like my scars are on the outside and I'm too disturbing to look at head-on.

So I leave proof of my existence behind me like a snail

trail with the small hope that years of talking *at* me will someday soften her enough to talk *with* me, that she'll finally pull the knife from my chest and say yes, we *are* better off without him. That what happened wasn't my fault and from now on she will thrust herself between me and danger, and shout *NO*.

Hands shaking, I fish a fresh cigarette from the front pocket of my bib overalls and try to light it off the old one. My chin trembles, the butts joust, and the burning head gets knocked off into the gutter at my feet.

I grind it out. Jab the unlit cigarette back into the pack.

Look up to see my mother's BMW pulling into the driveway.

A man sits shotgun.

My father.

chapter two

The driver's door opens and my mother pops out. She looks around expectantly and spots me hunkered on the curb instead of hurtling toward them, whooping, "Welcome home, Daddy!" Annoyance crimps her smile. "Meredith," she calls, waving me closer. "Look who's here!" Her scarlet nails glow orange in the sunset. "Come say hello!"

I can't. Breathing hurts and I want to run. His head turns toward me and my gaze jumps away, fixes on the fists filling my pockets. I count the rigid knuckles lumped beneath the faded denim. Four is my safe number. Eight is double strength. I smell terror in my sudden sweat. Oh God, please don't let this happen.

"Meredith," my mother says again, and there's steel beneath the honey. "I'm talking to you. Come here and say hello to your father, please. *Now.*"

It's the bitchy "now" that punctures my paralysis. *Now* he's here. *Now* she's happy. *Now* I'm supposed to act like nothing ever happened.

Anger saves me. I plant my palms on the curb and push myself up. Smooth my baggy overalls and black tank. Unhook my hair from behind my ears. The halves swing forward to curtain off all but my nose. My eyes burn and heat envelops my face.

The passenger door opens.

One sneakered foot is planted on the driveway. The other joins it.

The Nikes are blindingly new. Size twelve.

My mother has been shopping for him.

The jeans are also new. If I allow my gaze to travel higher—which I won't—I'll see the solid gold baseball charm on a chain that my mother gave him for his eighteenth birthday nestled in his coarse, whorled chest hair.

My front teeth throb as the memory of the charm bangs against them.

"Hello, Meredith."

The voice is quiet, kind, hoarse with history . . . and it destroys me. A sick, writhing knot of old love and despair lays me open worse than the first time and the force of it almost takes me down. I lock my knees, trying not to sway. This was not supposed to happen. I spent years steeling myself, reliving every rotten moment over and over again to make myself immune, hiding from nothing so there would be nothing hidden left to cripple me, and I thought

I'd made it, but now, with one simple greeting, I've already lost.

"No, Daddy, no. Don't."

"Meredith," he says again, soft and almost pleading, a voice I know, a voice that sends the nausea churning in my stomach straight up into my throat.

I swallow hard and lift my chin in reply. It's all I can manage and more than he deserves.

"Well." My mother plants her hands on her hips, peevish. "Is that the best welcome you can come up with? Why don't you come over here and give your father a hug?"

Hug him? *Touch* him? How can she even suggest it?

"It's okay. Don't push her, Sharon." He slams the passenger door and stretches, glances around the ominously silent court. Blinds twitch and a shade goes down, but he doesn't seem to notice. "Nice place. Peaceful. We have the rest of our lives to get reacquainted. Right, Chirp?"

My head jerks up, the curtain of hair parts, and for one piercing moment the predator and the prey lock gazes.

He winks at me before turning to my mother. "Don't worry, she'll come around. Three years is a long time to be out of a kid's life."

Not long enough! I want to shout, but I am mute, rooted in place as my stomach cramps and my defenses stumble in dazed disorder. He found me so easily. Resurrected my old nickname and broke right through. Does he know it? I don't know. So far I've only given him silence and surprise, so maybe he isn't sure. I have to count on that, have to believe I still have a chance to survive this.

"Yes, it is," my mother says, shooting me an exasperated look and shouldering her purse. "Why don't we go in out of this heat, Charles? I have some steaks defrosting—"

"No you don't." I come alive, reminded of my sabotage, and force myself up the lawn toward them. The grass is cool in the shade so I sit and make a show of removing my sandals. My feet are filthy from walking barefoot. I hitch up my pant leg and scratch my stubbly shin, making certain my father notes my horrible hygiene. I hate being dirty, but I know that he hates it more.

"Yes I do," my mother says, frowning. "I took three steaks out before I left."

"And I threw them away," I say, and nod at the Dumpster. "They smelled bad."

"What? All of them?" She is astonished. "Meredith, how could you?"

"They were rotten," I say with a careless shrug. "Probably loaded with E. coli, too. It's the stuff no one sees that does the most damage."

My father rubs his forehead, dulling the sweaty sheen above his brow.

"So you threw them away," my mother says, as if repeating it is the key to undoing it. "Sixty dollars' worth of steaks! How could they be rotten? I just bought them the other day!"

"Go smell for yourself," I say. "They're right on top."

She won't. He might, just to reassert his authority. I hope he does. The steaks are there, unwrapped and carefully laid out on top of a split garbage bag soggy with liquefied waste.

"Meredith, I don't . . . you know I . . . my *God* . . ." She's breathing hard, embarrassed and furious, caught between the harmonious, happy homecoming and letting me have it.

"Never mind, Shar," my father says, crossing around the front of the car and patting her back. His hand is awkward and although she turns from me and leans into him, he doesn't lean back. He worships youth. She chases it, but can never be young enough again. "I've been dreaming about Tony's pizzas for years. Come on, let's go order one."

Neither looks at me as they mount the front steps and fumble with the keys.

I stay where I am, silently counting the bricks in the steps and the cherry red geranium petals scattering the sidewalk beneath the urns flanking our porch. I count in lots of four, my gaze tracing corner-to-corner box shapes for each small group, and it isn't long before my heart slows and the trembling stops.

My parents will call Tony's and try to place a delivery order, but it'll be refused. Tony has caller ID and once he recognizes the last name, he'll say he doesn't deliver to our "area." He does, however, deliver to the rest of the complex. It's a daring discrimination, one that has earned my reluctant admiration.

My mother doesn't know Tony shuns us because she doesn't want to know.

But both she and my father are about to find out.

The good citizens of Estertown don't take kindly to child molesters or to the carrier families who deliberately host the virus and reinfect the community.

I glance across the court at the condo catty-cornered to my building.

Andy, who has ordered and received countless pizzas from Tony's for me, is sitting in his living room window. His bare chest gleams in the dying daylight. He shivers and lifts his bottle of Jim Beam in silent luck.

I nod because he sees, and knows.

chapter three

I slip through the front door in time to hear my mother's incredulous, "What do you mean you don't deliver to this area? Since when?"

Silence. The phone receiver crashes down.

"Well." My mother's voice is quick with indignation. "Apparently Tony doesn't care if he loses valuable customers!"

I wander into the kitchen entrance. My father is sitting at the table beneath his shimmering WELCOME HOME! banner. My mother stands by the fridge. The room is overcrowded and smells of soured nerves.

My mother spots me. "Meredith, did you know Tony's stopped delivering to our area?"

I turn away from her to the overhead cabinets. "Since when?" I say, removing my bottle of multivitamins. "I ordered a pie for lunch yesterday and they didn't have a problem delivering it." Actually, Andy had ordered it and we ate it together, but my parents don't know that and I see no

13

reason to tell them. "So why should they quit delivering to us now?"

The silence demands the obvious conclusion.

I remove my bottle of C vitamins, E, B complex. Flax seed oil, lecithin, calcium, lutein. Power supplements. Line them up in alphabetical order. Uncap them and shake one pill from each, recapping the bottles as I go.

"What're you doing?" my father asks.

I remain silent, taking a glass from the cabinet and focusing my attention on ensuring my survival.

"It's nice to see that your father's homecoming hasn't affected your little rituals," my mother says with spite, but she reaches into the fridge and hands me a cold can of V8 anyway. "She won't talk when she's taking her vitamins. I don't know why, so don't even ask." Her laugh is strained. "I'm sorry, Charles, I didn't mean to snap. I just wanted everything to go so smoothly for your homecoming and instead it's such a . . ." She stops, breathing deeply to compose herself. "You're home again and that's all that matters."

I cough, then continue swallowing vitamins. Four pills, four sips of vegetable juice. Four is the number of reality, logic, and reason plus the essence of mind, body, and spirit brought to the material plane to form a square. It's a strong number, one with substance, and I've felt safe in it ever since that first night in the hospital.

"You know, there's something I've been wanting to do and now seems like the perfect time," my father says.

The vitamins rattle in my cupped hand. I put them in my mouth and swallow.

Chair legs scrape the floor and his sneakers squeal as he rounds the table.

If he touches me—traps me in his arms and pulls me against him—if that golden baseball nudges my skull and his belt buckle brands my spine, then—

A muffled, sucking sound breaks my panic.

"Oh no, Charles," my mother protests. "It's your first night home!"

"It's fine," he says. "I need to get back into the swing of things anyway and besides, I want to see if I've lost my touch. Now, what do we have in here to work with?"

Frigid air sweeps my ankles and I risk a glance over my shoulder.

My father's rummaging through the freezer.

Memories flash and I see him in our old house's kitchen. . . .

His legs sprout from beneath faded shorts and the golden baseball swings around his neck. We've just come in from outside, where he's been teaching me how to play softball. "Don't take it so hard, Chirp. We'll try again tomorrow—"

I slump against the wall and stare at my dusty sneakers. My fingers ache and my palms are blistered. "I wanted to get a hit today."

My bottom lip trembles. "If I got a hit, then you would like me the way you like the boys who get hits."

He goes still. "How do I like the boys?"

"Better," I say, wanting to sound snotty, but my voice crumbles.

"Hey, don't cry." He crouches and draws me close between his knees. Strokes my back as I burrow into the hollow between his neck and shoulder. "You're my girl. I'll always like you better than any old boys."

"Really?" My voice is muffled and my mouth moves against his salty skin. He tastes like a giant pretzel. This amuses me and I pretend to bite him, raking my new rabbit teeth across his skin and giggling. "Yum, you taste good, Daddy."

He pulls me tighter, but his body is suddenly too hot.

I squirm free. "How many strikes do I get before I'm out?"

My father rises and turns away. "Three," he says, and his voice is gruff. "That sound good, Chirp?"

"That sound good, Chirp?"

I jam the last four vitamins into my mouth and guzzle the rest of the juice. It dribbles down my chin, splashes the front of my shirt. I don't wipe it off.

"Meredith, your father's talking to you," my mother says. "He's going to barbecue chicken. Doesn't that sound delicious?"

I lean past her and plunk the glass in the sink. "I'm going out."

"Out?" my father says. "Now? What about dinner?"

"I already ate," I say, running the faucet. The cold water bubbles into the glass and gushes back up, splattering the stainless steel. I ignore it, knowing my mother will attack the droplets before they can dry and leave unsightly spots.

"Stop it, you're making a mess," she snaps, reaching around me and turning off the water. "What is *wrong* with you today?" She grabs a dishtowel and looks down at her new dress, splashed across the belly where she's leaned up against the spattered countertop. "Oh no, this is silk! It's not supposed to get wet!" She blots frantically at the spots. "I hope you're satisfied, Meredith. Welcome home, Charles!" She throws the towel on the floor, bursts into tears, and clatters from the room.

Her bedroom door slams. It doesn't lock, though, and the implied invitation throbs in the silence.

"That wasn't a very nice thing to do," my father says after a moment, making no move to follow her. "If you're mad at me, don't take it out on her."

"I rinsed a glass," I say in a monotone, and turn to leave because my father and I are not supposed to be alone together, ever, and we all know it.

"Wait," my father says, rising and crossing the kitchen. He retrieves the crumpled towel and lays it on the counter next to where I'm standing. Casually blocks my path as I try to slip around him. "Come on now, what's with you? I know it's been a while, but it's not like I'm a stranger." And then, softer, "Are you holding a grudge against me? If you are, then we're gonna have to work it through because I am home to stay."

His heat sparks the dry kindling in my chest and I stand helpless, eyes closed behind the hair curtaining my face, trapped between him and the firestorm. . . .

"Mmm, dessert time." My father brings a teaspoon of sweet baby custard toward my mouth. "Open up, Mer."

I do, wiggling and banging my hands on the highchair tray.

He chuckles. "You look just like a hungry baby bird." Leans over and kisses my nose. "You're a charmer, little chirpy bird."

I burble and open my mouth for more. . . .

"It hurts that you never came to see me," he says quietly, touching my arm. "Three years is a long time. Don't you think we should forgive each other and move on? I love you, you know. That has to count for something."

My blood boils beneath his fingers. One by one, the vessels split, sear, and shrink away. If I don't release myself, I will spontaneously combust.

"C'mon," he says, and it's not his wheedling tone or his plea for forgiveness that sickens me. It's the look I catch when I peer through the curtain, the way his thumb is rubbing soft, rhythmic circles on my arm. "How about giving your old man a break here, huh, Chirp?"

"Chirp is dead," I hear myself say and watch the flat words destroy his pleasure. "You killed her, and now you have to deal with me because I'm what's left." I push past him and walk out the front door into the gathering dusk.

chapter four

I hesitate, heart pounding, and when he doesn't follow, hurry around the blind side of the condo. We have the last unit next to the Dumpster court.

Bad things are happening. It's not my imagination and it's not paranoia. It's real. My gut hasn't stopped roiling since he got here, and it's not because of the past. I know every inch of what's done; what scares me is what *he* seems to know is coming.

I think of my mother throwing that fit and flouncing off, expecting my father to follow and comfort her in the privacy of her boudoir. He didn't, though, at least not in the moment that mattered, and that's not good.

I need to move so I run past Andy's mother's creaky, ancient Cadillac squatting like a broad-hipped hussy in all her Civil War-esque mottled blue and primer-gray glory. The condo association hates this car, claims its presence negatively affects the quality of life here at Cambridge Oaks, and has been searching for a way to ban it from the complex, but just like the Dumpster lid, the car thwarts them. It's inspected, registered, and insured, and there are no ordinances—yet—prohibiting ugly vehicles from parking amidst glossy ones.

What they don't know—and don't seem to care about—is that Ms. Mues has a valid reason for driving a clunker. It's the perfect nosy-neighbor repellant. Everyone ignores her because at Cambridge Oaks, the only thing worse than the presence of a junk car is the possibility of someone noticing you talking to its owner.

Andy opens the door as I reach the top of his back steps.

The porch light burned out over a year ago on the day they moved in, Andy arriving on a stretcher, fresh from graduating Estertown High and becoming a tragic statistic. His mother told me she took the sudden darkness as a sign from Jesus and will not go against His will by lighting a path He's seen fit to cast into shadows.

Andy's mother worships Jesus the way Memphis worships Elvis.

"I saw," Andy says. His pupils are black wells rimmed with irises the color of walnut shells and his skin is moon-pale because he rarely leaves the house. He scans my face and backs up to let me in.

"I know," I say, slipping into the dark, smoky kitchen. Scented candles and patchouli incense flicker in a dozen places. "I need to take a shower. Bad."

"Go for it," he says, as if this is a perfectly normal request. "Just move all the stuff out of the way."

"Thanks." I slip past him and down the shadowy hall. Ms. Mues's bedroom is opposite the bathroom, but it's Friday and her door is shut, so I don't bother her.

Andy's bathroom has the same layout as ours, but that's where the similarity ends. Instead of fluffy white towels, marble tiles, and a whirlpool tub, their bathroom has worn green carpet and a fish shower curtain hanging crooked off the rod. But it's clean and there's patchouli soap, so I move the chair out of the tub, undress, and spend a grateful five minutes scrubbing the feel of my father's fingers off my skin.

I count the wall tiles as I dry off, first absently and then with growing concern. The numbers are unsettling, with blocks of four leaving a row of strays totaling one horizontally or seven vertically.

One is the primary number from which all others grow. It's an upsurge of power and the beginning of all things. One is the first day of the week. One is the loneliest number.

Seven, on the other hand, is the number of completion. Seven deadly sins, seven virtues, seven vices. On the seventh day, God rested.

The odd numbers disturb me, so I stuff my towel in the hamper and return to the kitchen.

Andy turns from watching out the back door window. "All clear."

"Good." I head for the smoldering incense and cup my hands, pulling the rich, earthy scent over me four times. I'm not self-conscious about it; Andy knows almost all of me, has explored my private places and tended my bruises. There's little I could do to drive him away. "Want to order a pizza? I'll buy."

"It's Friday," he reminds me, flipping his braid back over his shoulder. "There are two slices left from yesterday. I'll warm them up for you." He motions me into a seat and rolls his wheelchair to the fridge.

I sit in my regular spot and watch as he removes a paper plate from the lowest shelf. I'll be the only one eating tonight; Friday is fasting day and Ms. Mues allows nothing but wounded souls and spirits to enter her home while she and Andy undergo purification. I light a cigarette and blow rings that dissolve upon impact with the incense smoke. "So what do you think?" I ask.

Andy puts the pizza in the microwave. He turns to face me and his eyes blur with sorrow. He grips the Jim Beam bottle tucked into the V of his groin, lifts it, and drinks.

Now I know it's going to be bad.

He wedges the bottle back between his thighs and rolls toward me. Stops when we're knee to knee and takes my free hand. Bows his head, murmurs a soft prayer. Releases me and sits back. "Your father's not reformed or repentant, Mer. He's *eager*. He's gone without for three years and he's hungrier now than he was before." His bare shoulders twitch and goose bumps pox his skin. "Sooner or later he's gonna want to get off and not with your mom, you know? He hardly even looked at her. It's all about you."

I nod, vaguely nauseous, and draw on my cigarette. Burn my lips on the close heat and stub the filter out in the ashtray. "He says he loves me. I was hoping I'd be too old for him now. I mean, I look different, I smell different . . . but when he called me Chirp, I knew." I light a second cigarette. "It's not over. He said we should forgive and get on with our lives, like I'm partly to blame! And then he tries to lay a guilt trip on me by telling me it hurt because I wouldn't go see him in prison." I jerk my fist and the smoke trail arcs. "I felt like saying, 'Good, I'm glad it hurt. I hope it kills you.' But I didn't because he was smiling, Andy. He was enjoying it."

The spokes in Andy's wheelchair twinkle as he crosses the kitchen and brings me my pizza. "What did your mother say?"

"She's useless," I say, sprinkling salt from the three holes bored in the top of the Virgin Mary's head on the slices. Joseph is pepper, less generous with only two holes. The ceramic figures do double work as Ms. Mues uses them in her mantelpiece manger scene at Christmas. I've never had the heart to tell her that five is the number of uncertainty.

Andy sets a paper cup of tap water down by my napkin.

"Thank you. I can't count on her at all," I say, chewing each bite eight times. "At least your mother *did* something when she found out. Mine won't even acknowledge it. She keeps calling it a mistake, like it was nothing more than taking a wrong turn somewhere. She's acting like everything's fine and nothing ever happened, like all this time my father's been off on some business trip instead of locked up in prison. I hate it."

"I thought you guys were getting a new social worker," Andy says, taking the plate as I gnaw the last of the sauce from the crusts.

"We're supposed to meet with someone next week, but you know what a joke that is. They'll read the history and go over the same stuff, ask me if everything's okay—"

"Yeah, right in front of your parents, so what're you supposed to say? 'No, get this sick bastard out of my house before he starts again'?" Andy snorts. "And why do you even have to *say* it? I mean, c'mon, they already know he's an equal opportunity molester, it's all in the file; you, the boys. . . ."

"Actually, I found some psych stuff online about

crossover offending. Going after any kid that moves no matter if it's a boy or a girl, I mean." I grimace and wipe my mouth. "How bad is it that there's actually an official category for guys like him? I mean, how many are there anyway?" I rise and throw my napkin in the garbage. "All I can say is they chose to let him out in three instead of nine and if anything happens to me, I swear it's on them."

Three, the number of growth and expansion, the result of one and two.

Three strikes. Three is a crowd.

"All right," Andy says quietly. "Come on."

I follow him out of the kitchen and back down the hallway. The light's off and won't be turned on again until after midnight, but I've walked this route a hundred times, counting my steps and the whispery, whirring revolutions of Andy's wheels.

And I wonder, not for the first time, how Ms. Mues can dwell in darkness fifty-two times a year and still see so clearly while my own mother, a creature of sunlight and shine, sees nothing at all.

We crowd into the bathroom to wash our hands. Close the door so as not to disturb his mother, who is still secluded in her bedroom, communing with Jesus and anyone else who decides to show up.

Andy works well in the dark. His soapy hands move

gently over my skin, up and down between my fingers, around my wrists. He doesn't talk while he cleanses, but I can hear him breathing.

We're not afraid of the dark. Our nightmares were born on sultry, summer afternoons. I was three when my father, Estertown's middle school gym teacher and favorite softball coach, left my mother and moved in on the other side of town with Paula Mues Beecher, a widow with a sad, shy seven-year-old son.

I don't remember those days.

Andy does, vividly. For him it was the beginning of the end.

"Done," he says and rinses my hands with warm water.

"Thank you," I say and lean slowly, blindly into the abyss. Our noses bump, shift, and accommodate. I can feel his goatee and his smile against my lips.

His arms circle my waist. I pick up his bottle and ease down onto his lap.

We roll to his bedroom.

chapter five

A ndy's room smells like a fresh grave in June.

He burns the same patchouli candles as his mother, but in this shadowy space their scent mingles with the sweet musk of damask roses and makes me think of sun-warmed petals scattered by mourners to honor a passing.

There are no live flowers in Andy's house and there haven't been for as long as I've known him. The rose scent has no foundation and no traceable source. It doesn't increase or decrease. It just is.

The Mueses accept it without question and believe it's a gift of benevolent grace.

I have no blind faith, no one to thank for mysterious gifts, so sometimes I crawl around, sniffing the floor vents and searching for hidden plug-in fresheners.

There never are any, of course.

I climb off Andy's bony legs and place the bottle on his nightstand next to the sturdy, oaken Madonna icon. She looms three feet tall, a testament to devotion, and gazes at me in mute radiance, hands gently clasped and lips curved in a beatific smile.

Ms. Mues is certain that one day the Holy Mother's serene eyes will weep shimmering oil tears and, in her infinite mercy, will bestow a long-awaited miracle on Andy. She believes his recovery will occur via a victim soul, a pious individual chosen by the divine to absorb and endure the pain and suffering of others.

I listen carefully and because I like Ms. Mues, I don't point out that Andy feels no pain from his paralysis or that my definition of mercy does not include picking specific humans to be clearinghouses for all sorts of mortal agonies.

Ms. Mues must read it in my eyes, though, because she laughs and tells me not to worry, that God works in mysterious ways. How else would I explain this condo going vacant right after Andy's accident and in time for them to rent, or our deep and immediate bond, if it wasn't all a part of some grander plan?

I don't know. I could mention that my old friend Azzah's family, the previous tenants, were evicted for cramming too much exuberant, extended family into the two-bedroom condo and not being savvy enough to be quiet about it, but that still doesn't account for what happened when Andy and I first saw each other. . . .

I sit on the curb, the June sun baking my brain, a disposable lighter in hand and a pile of notes at my feet. The notes have come once a week, every week, for almost two years now, tucked inside the letters addressed to my mother, all bearing the same New Jersey State Prison return address. Every week after my mother devours her letter she reads mine and then hands it over, waiting for me to read it. Every week I take it into my room and throw it in the gray storage tub I keep in the back of the closet.

And once a year on the anniversary date, while my mother is off designing window displays, I gather those unread notes and pile them on the pavement near the Dumpster.

Then I light them and watch them burn.

I flick the lighter, lower my hand, and touch the first note. It blackens and crumbles in on itself, igniting the page beneath.

A transport ambulance followed by an enormous old Cadillac cruises slowly around the bend and heads for our lot. The ambulance stops at the curb in front of the empty condo and two EMS guys get out. They leave the engine running and the faint strains of Los Lonely Boys' "Heaven" in their wake. They glance at me, at the crackling flames at my feet, and exchange speaking looks.

I avert my gaze and watch as the Cadillac creeps into a parking spot. When I look back, the EMS techs have rounded the ambulance and opened the rear doors. One guy climbs in; the other begins pulling out the stretcher.

There's a body shape under the sheet.

I feel weird now, like some gross rubbernecker ogling an accident, so I quickly pour the last of my bottled water onto the fire's charred remains and rise to leave.

As I do, the person on the stretcher comes into sight.

Pale, gaunt. Dark eyes shadowed beneath sleepy lids, gaze bleak. Brown hair cloaking his shoulders, a battered wooden cross on a leather thong around his neck.

He looks right at me.

The world blurs and a great rushing fills my ears. The pit of my stomach throbs, my skin tingles with immediate heat. Jesus, he's beautiful. And his mouth is moving. What's he saying? I don't know, I can't hear—

"Honey, are you all right? You look like you're going to pass out."

I draw a sharp breath and the world swoops back. A woman I've never seen before has me by the arm and is peering worriedly into my face. "I'm fine," I stammer, mortified, not daring to look at the stretcher. "I think I got up too fast." I step back and she releases me, but her grasp still pulses against my skin. "Thanks. I . . . I have to go."

But somehow I don't and instead find myself invited in, following this woman up the steps and through the back door as the bulb in the porch light pops, as the EMS guys wheel the stretcher across the lawn and into the condo through the sliding glass.

And somehow he and I end up alone together in the living room while the woman signs off on the transport. The heat is unbearable, the silence stifling. He fingers his cross, turns his face away, and I stand there sweating, searching for something to break this stale-mate—

"You never answered my question," he says, still without looking at me. "What were you burning when we pulled up?"

I shouldn't tell him. I shouldn't. He'll think I'm pathetic. "Letters," I hear myself say. "From someone I never want to see again for as long as I live."

He looks at me now and in that raw heartbeat, something more passes between us, something fierce and too intense to be spoken. He nods, pulls himself up to a sitting position, and gestures to the end of the bed. "You might as well take a seat and—"

"Make yourself at home," Andy says, closing and locking his door.

Smiling, I sink onto the bed and crawl up to the head-board. Light the incense, prop a pillow, and watch as he wheels to the media cabinet. Old scars zigzag his bare back and chest, intersecting like cross streets down his arms and along his hands. I've traveled them all from source to desti-nation, committing his history to memory and learning him from the outside in.

"I want you to hear something," he says, sticking a CD into the player. "All these years of looking and I finally found it on eBay for like five bucks. I can't believe nobody else bid on it." His braid has grown past the middle of his back and when he sweats, it sticks to the vinyl back of his chair. "You're going to like it, Mer. Just give it a chance."

The CD starts and it's Dean Martin crooning "Little Green Apples." I almost groan, but Andy looks so entranced that I hold back. He's raved about this song forever, struggling to remember the lyrics, telling me how his late father had loved it, too, humming the few strains he could recall. This song is his personal, private soundtrack, the way "Heaven" has become mine, and the least I can do is keep an open mind.

Or maybe my response is completely selfish because I know that as the love song gentles Andy, he will, in turn, gentle me.

. . . Little green apples . . .

Andy smiles.

Dino's voice can do in seconds what quarts of Jim Beam can't do in days.

He hoists himself out of his chair and into bed beside me. His skin is parchment in the soft light and his eyes are hooded, black hollows. He unclips my overall straps and folds down the bib. Waits until I take off my shirt, then rests his head on my stomach and sighs. "God, what a voice. I wish I could sing."

"I wish you could sing, too," I tease, pleased by his sudden snort of laughter.

"Wise guy." His coarse goatee moves against me with each word. "I love this song, Mer. No angst. No craziness. It just is what it is."

"Corny," I murmur, to keep him talking. I like the way his chin grazes my belly and his breath wisps across me like warm satin. Inhale. Exhale. The rhythm settles deep inside me and I shift my hips.

He runs a hand up my leg and nudges into the front of my baggy overalls, coming to rest on the low slope between my hipbones. "You were in my dream last night," he says and kisses my belly button.

"Good or bad?" I say, watching him in the floor-to-ceiling tiled mirror across from the bed. There are thirty-two tiles in all, four across and eight down, and they provide an interesting angle; I see the ends of us before the beginnings. The soles of my feet are still dirty and dissolve into the shadows. Andy's bare, bloodless feet tangle to-gether in a heap.

"Well, it was definitely weird," he says, dipping his fin-gers out of sight beneath my overalls. He hasn't touched anything vital yet, but he's close, and his voice grows husky with the knowledge. He tilts his head back to look at me and my breast blinds him. Smiling, he props himself up on an elbow, pulls his braid over his shoulder, and tugs off the band. "You were sitting on this stone wall—"

"Where?" I interrupt.

"I don't know, but there were these funky flowers all around that smelled like cotton candy," he says. "I was standing in the dark watching you, wondering why I was stuck inside while you were out there looking all golden, so I just decided the hell with it and walked out to meet you. I actually heard my own footsteps on the stones." He glances at me. "You know what you said when I got there?"

I shake my head.

"You were reading a dictionary—"

"A *dictionary?* Oh, come on. I don't even own a dictionary."

"And you looked up and said, *'Now* I get it,' and closed the book." His gaze holds a silent plea. "It was all so real. I mean, I was sweating and shaking and when I sat down next to you, the edge of the wall cut into the backs of my legs. It wasn't a memory because I didn't know you when I could still walk. Do you think it was a vision?"

I don't know anything about visions and I'm pretty sure paraplegia can't be reversed, so I don't answer him, just lean forward and slip off my bra. It's a B cup, black like the soles of my feet, like the anticipation in his eyes. Black lace via Victoria's Secret and five minutes alone with my mother's charge card.

"You know about victim souls, right?" Andy asks as I scooch back against the headboard and draw up my knees, giving him a wall to lean against while I brush out his soft, rippling hair.

"I know they're supposed to be pious people—whatever that means—and that your mother wants to find one who'll absorb your suffering and bless you with recovery," I say, separating the silky strands and shivering as they drift across my bare skin. I stroke his hair, trace his scars. His accident-prone days are over. I pick up the brush on the nightstand.

"Right," he says, watching me watch him in the mirror. "Well, there's one out in Iowa. An old disabled guy who receives messages from the Virgin Mary. My mother's going to make a pilgrimage out there."

"That would be good for her," I say.

"I'm going, too," he says quietly.

I stop brushing. "To Iowa?"

"Yeah," he says.

I gaze at our reflection, at my bare shoulders rising from behind my drawn-up knees, at the translucence of his skin and the tension tightening his features. "You're going to Iowa." Repeating it makes me want to hurt him. "When?"

"We leave on Sunday," he says to the expressionless girl in the mirror.

"This Sunday? Like day-after-tomorrow Sunday?" I say, sitting up straight. "Why now? What's the big rush?"

"My mother put my name on the waiting list over a year ago," he says. "They finally called last night: We'll have an hour with him on Monday and another one on Tuesday morning." An odd, fleeting expression grips his features. They smooth again, but not before realization knuckles a cold fist into my stomach.

"You *want* to go," I say and my hands scramble furiously, separating his hair into three thick strands and reweaving, yanking each over-under pass, jerking his head back again and again until his gaze in the mirror glazes with tears.

I stop, defeated by his acceptance of my punishment. "Andy." I can't say more. I haven't begged for anything since Chirp's thighs were yanked apart like a Thanksgiving wishbone.

"If I don't take this appointment I'll have to wait another year," he says, shifting and pulling himself up alongside of me. He runs his hand down my spine and lingers at the small of my back. "I already asked." He reaches past me for the bottle of Jim Beam and uncaps it. Drinks and coughs when he's finished. "I know it's bad timing, but I can't wait anymore, Mer. Something's got to give."

"There is no such thing as miracles, Andy," I say.

He leans away and cool air rushes to fill the absence.

I twist to look at him and the stubborn hope blurring his face pushes me further, makes me want to gouge holes in his faith. "I mean, come on, if the Blessed Virgin has such infinite mercy, then how can she listen to your prayers every day for years without doing something about them?"

He upends the bottle. Wipes his mouth. "Maybe she is."

I grab my bra. My hands are palsied and I hate them for it.

"We'll be back on Wednesday," he says.

"Have a nice trip," I say, sliding the straps up onto my shoulders.

"I'll give you my keys." His hands cover mine, which are struggling to hook my bra. "I wouldn't leave you here with nowhere to go."

I stop battling my underwear. "Four days is a long time."

"I know." He rubs soft circles on my back.

I close my eyes against the Believe poster taped to his closet door. "Anything could happen," I say, surrendering to the rhythm of his warm strength. His hands slip 'round to nudge my bra aside.

"Come here if it gets bad. You'll be safe." His sigh stirs my hair. "I promise."

I look at the oaken Madonna. Her face is serene, her gaze a caress. Silently I ask why she'd send him all the way to Iowa now, while my father's on the loose, but although I listen hard for an answer, the Blessed Virgin isn't talking.

Andy is, though. His mouth is against my ear and his hand is in my overalls.

I reach up behind me and pull his braid forward, unbanding and spreading the rippling strands down over his shoulders. Down over my face. The curtain closes and I open. His reach is blind but accurate.

"Two," I whisper, pressing my teeth against his cheek and taking fistfuls of his hair. Two's a good number, one for me and one for him, pleasure evenly divided.

"Four," he counters, a smile in his voice.

I forgive his approaching abandonment. I forgive him for not being what I want and am thankful for his being what I need. I open my eyes and gaze up into his face. His pleasure is giving me pleasure and I would not disappoint him.

"You know I love you," he says.

The room smells of roses and freshly turned dirt.

"Andy," I say, buffeted by the rush.

And then again.

"Andy."

chapter six

My self-imposed curfew on purification Fridays is 11:30 P.M. Leaving Andy's before midnight when his mother ends her exile is easier on us all. There really *is* such a thing as too much information, and when I ease from his lingering grasp and slip out into the night I am, with my friction-knotted hair and bruised lips, walking proof of this. One look and Ms. Mues would have the answer to a question she's deliberately never asked.

I pause on the back porch, shrouded in darkness. The metal steps are cool under my feet. The night air is thick with moisture and ratcheting cricket songs.

" . . . the hell is she? It's almost midnight."

"Relax, Charles." My mother's voice carries a thread of impatience. "She'll be back. She's a big girl, you know."

I lean out over the rail just far enough to peek around the corner of the building. My parents are sitting on our front porch, my mother in the center of the step, my father pressed up against the railing. His shoulders are hunched forward like he's going to launch himself the moment I come into view. Only problem is he's staring in the wrong direction.

Silence. And then icily, "She's a fifteen-year-old *child,* Sharon."

My mother laughs and leans against him. "I was only twelve when we got together, remember?"

His head snaps around toward her and although I can't see his expression, the startled flash zapping my mother's face speaks volumes. "She's *my child* and I'm not going to sit by and let her run wild doing who knows what with who knows *who.* I'm putting the brakes on this tonight." His voice is rising and my mother touches his arms, shushing him. He shrugs away.

Air conditioners thrum and lights glow behind shades. The complex is a tomb, haunted only by the Shale family and the Dumpster's putrid miasma.

Whap!

"The mosquitoes are eating me alive," my mother says.

"So go inside," he says, keeping his gaze pinned on the blind curve of the main road. "I'm staying here."

My mother pouts and scratches her ankle, but doesn't surrender her spot.

I climb soundlessly over the opposite railing and drop to the grass. Pad through shadows, heading away from the court and my building, taking the long way up around

Andy's building so that I'll come out above the blind curve. I would be a fool to go straight home from Andy's, to reveal my sanctuary to the serpent.

I fish a cigarette from the pack and pause to light it. My father will smell the smoke on my breath the moment I open my mouth. He'll also smell pizza, patchouli incense, maybe even the tangy scent of Andy's mouth, moist with Jim Beam, anointing my skin.

I pick up my pace. *His child.* Right. Maybe I was once, but not anymore.

Andy's pending departure makes me feel grimly reckless. It's like he's confirmed what I've always known but never gave voice to; when it comes to nightmares, we are each truly on our own.

I pause above the blind curve near the front of the complex. My father's new condo is in Building A and I can see it from where I'm standing.

If I had a big old rotten tomato, I'd splat it against his front door.

Maybe I will tomorrow night while he's submitting to my mother's determined seduction. With her urchin hair and face stripped of makeup she may actually get somewhere as long as the lights are out and his imagination is active.

And providing there's a daughter lying sleepless in the bedroom across the hall, bearing unwilling witness.

I take a deep drag on my cigarette. Flick the ashes.

In my dream, I am bouncing along a path with Tigger. We boing up and land with a booming thud and a springy eeee. The noises split my dream and I crawl up and out of the woods . . .

Thud, thud, thud.

I climb out of bed and go to my door. A light shines at the end of the black tunnel where shadows rise and fall on the walls.

I enter the darkness. The night-light is off. I'm supposed to call 911 for bad things, but I go down the hall to my mother instead.

Heart thundering, I edge to the brink of the open door.

My mother is on her knees on the bed.

My father's face is crunched up and his hair is wet on his fore-head.

I am paralyzed. My mother has never said to call 911 on my fa-ther.

He spots me, gaze burning, and puts a finger to his lips.

I back up a step, wanting to run to my room.

He shakes his head, makes a "wait" sign. Watches me watch him, nails my feet to the floor, and makes my chest ache for air.

Thudthudthudthudthud!

My father's eyes roll back. I'm terrified because he's gone into an ep-il-ep-tic fit like old Mrs. Nelson's collie Boyd always does. I dash back to my room, bury myself under the covers, and then my father crouches near my bed whispering that I'm a brave girl and if I ever hear noises like that again I should come see what's wrong like I did tonight, to watch quiet as a mouse and make sure that my mother is safe, but never to let her see me because it will be our secret . . .

I pretend to be asleep until he leaves.

The next night the noises go on and on and I realize that they'll never stop unless I do what my father has said. So I do and when it ends my feet are no longer nailed to the floor and we've kept my mother safe for another night.

The next afternoon I'm playing in old Mrs. Nelson's kitchen with her collie Boyd and he goes into an ep-il-ep-tic fit and I watch, quiet as a mouse, to make sure he stays safe.

Two nights later when the thudding starts, I rise and drag into the hallway. I don't put it off anymore because I don't want my mother to suffer any longer than she has to. This time she sees me at the brink of the shadows.

"Meredith! Charles, stop!" She pulls away and covers herself. Whips a pillow in front of him. "Meredith! What's wrong?"

"I heard a noise," I mumble, staring at my feet. I didn't know she could get away so easily and now I feel stupid.

"It's all right, everything's fine," my mother says, wrapping the sheet around her. "Let's get you back to bed."

"Mommy," I whisper, as she leans over to kiss me. "Are you safe?"

Her eyes flicker. "Of course I am. I have you and Daddy to protect me."

"Good." I snuggle down, satisfied that my father hasn't lied to me . . .

Fool. I peer through the smoke at his condo and wish I had a whole bushel of tomatoes right now. I'd whip them at his door, watching each burst into a scarlet heap of—

"Haven't seen you in a while, Meredith."

Inside, my stomach jumps. Outside, I turn to meet Nigel Balthazar and his enormous, white Great Pyrenees, Gilly. Nigel is a retired Estertown cop and lives in a building near my father's. My parents don't know this and, once again, I see no reason to enlighten them.

"I've been around," I say, relaxing and tucking my hair behind my ears. "At Andy's mostly. My grandmother's once or twice. She's been trying to talk my mother into letting me stay with her over the summer, but my father wants me home and of course his wish is my mother's command." I shrug and scratch the top of Gilly's Plymouth Rock head.

She wags her tail and washes my arm with her tongue.

"Hmph. Figures. Andy okay these days?" Nigel asks, jabbing a Winston into his mouth and rummaging through his shirt pocket for his lighter. The windproof flame tints his weathered face a sheer tangerine. He lifts his head, exhaling.

"I guess," I say, flicking my cigarette into the gutter. "He's leaving for Iowa on Sunday with his mother. They have an appointment with a victim soul."

"What, one of those religious rainmakers? Christ, those

46

two. Hard heads, both of them. That kid needs a good shrink and some physical therapy, not some corn-fed quack quoting Scriptures and waving a crucifix." Nigel squints at me through the spiraling smoke. "It's lousy timing for you, but I'll keep a good thought for our boy. Who knows, maybe it'll pay off and he can send that chair back to the old folks' home where it belongs."

One of the things Nigel and I have in common is loving Andy. The other is knowing far too much about my father, his past, and probable future.

"I hear your old man's out," he says and taps the cellphone wedged into his shirt pocket. "Boys on the force say he hasn't been down to register yet."

"He hasn't? Well, I'll have to remind him then." My lips twitch at the thought.

"That why you're out so late?" he says, hitching up his pants. He wears old man jeans that hang low under his belly, brown slipper moccasins, and a faded plaid shirt that does nothing to soften the edges of his solid bulk.

"Pretty much. He's at my house right now, waiting for me to get home so he can 'put the brakes' on my disappearing act." I glance at my father's building. "He's in A-Eight."

"I know." Nigel's eyes narrow. "Hear from social services?"

"Next week, but what can they do? He's out and he's here. So he makes my life miserable, so what? Nobody cares. If they did they would never have released him." I blink hard and my vision clears. The tears surprise me; I haven't cried in years.

"He get out of line with you yet?"

I shrug. "He cornered me and said we should forgive each other. And he called me . . . Chirp." The once-innocent nickname shrivels my tongue.

Nigel swears briefly. "You gonna be able to handle this on your own?"

I think of Andy's pending absence and my mother's deliberate blind spot. My grandmother's still an option, but she leads a very busy life and she and my mother have never really gotten along. I know she hates my father, though; I once heard her say that child molesters were often murdered in prison and she'd sounded very hopeful. I'm pretty sure she'll help me if I need it.

"It's gonna be bad," Nigel says, watching me.

"Good. Then maybe he'll leave," I reply.

"I meant bad for you," he says.

"I'm not helpless anymore," I say, and almost believe it.

chapter seven

Nigel and Gilly peel off in one direction and I go in the other.

I head back with the comfort of knowing that Nigel will watch out for me until I disappear around the bend. Once I do, I'm no more than a Hail Mary pass from home.

I glance at my watch. The witching hour has come and gone. My father should be livid by now. I swing my hair forward, anticipating the confrontation.

It feels good to be back to the original plan.

I am going to drive him out of here and away from me.

Be everything he hates. Use every tool I have.

I round the bend and see my parents perched like over-size vultures on the front porch. They snap to attention as I pass beneath a streetlight. I slip my hands into my overall pockets and feel my thighs flexing beneath my palms. My knees have lost their rubbery feeling and I think of Andy as I left him tonight; eyes closed and fists striking his own lifeless legs, calling for the Virgin's mercy, asking the Mystical Rose, Mother undefiled, Mirror of justice, Comforter of the afflicted to intercede and relay his plea to her Son. Begging her to ask Him, in the name of love, for restoration.

So Andy hides and prays while I trudge back into the fire, leaking flammable memories.

God, what a mess.

I cross the warm macadam, hoping I look scornful and bored. Step onto my neatly edged, postage-stamp front lawn and amble up to the porch where they wait.

"Meredith," my father says, rising.

His summons almost stops me, but I make myself sweep past him and up the steps. "You guys are nutty for sitting out here. The mosquitoes are brutal."

"We've been waiting for *you.*" His voice is tight. "You look like hell. Where have you been?"

"Out." My hand closes around the doorknob.

" 'Out' where?" he says.

The door opens and I shrug as I pass through it. "Just out." I walk inside and give it a shove after me.

My father blocks it and follows me in. My mother is his shadow. "Please don't walk away from me when I'm talking to you, Meredith."

I exhale a hearty sigh and stop. "What?"

"You didn't answer my question," he says. "Where were you tonight?"

"Out," I say.

" 'Out' is not an acceptable answer," he snaps.

"It was until today," I drawl.

"Well, it's not anymore," he says, giving my flushed mother an accusing look. "You can't just disappear without telling us where you're going or who you're going to be with and you can't come wandering in at all hours of the night looking like you've been—"

"Raped?" The foyer is too small for the ringing silence. "Not to worry. Estertown's been safe for three years now, *Dad.*" I push past them both.

No one speaks.

I go into my room and lock the door. Look in the mirror for a long time until the trembling stops, until I hear the front door slam and the deadbolt slide home.

Watch from the window as my father strides down the road toward his condo.

I wait, but my mother doesn't come to me.

Miserable, I undress and crawl into bed.

chapter eight

I wake up Saturday morning with the dogged hope that my father has somehow died overnight, that a bulging aneurysm has popped and bled him out or that his heart simply stopped beating.

There are other ways for him to die, of course, but these two absolve me of everything but hope and a person can't be jailed for hoping. At least that's what my old therapist said when she told me my anger was normal and should be voiced. She would have told me more, I'm sure, but my mother stopped our visits after my second "unpleasant venting."

I ease out of bed, cross the carpeted floor, and listen at the door.

The condo is quiet. A hint of coffee lingers but it's faint and not fresh.

Nothing. No TV, no voices, no blathering morning radio.

I slip across the hall to the bathroom. Pee and flush.

Rinse my face in hot water. The countertop gets splattered with the runoff from my elbows and I give it a cursory swipe with my mother's scarlet guest towel. The lace is scratchy and not absorbent.

I tuck back my hair and head for the kitchen. Freeze in the entranceway.

"Good morning," my father says, glancing up from the newspaper spread out across the table. "I hope I didn't startle you." His gaze scans my thigh-high sleep T. "There's orange juice in the fridge—"

"Where's my mother?" Panic sharpens my voice.

"She ran to the deli to get bagels," he says, leaning back in the chair. "We thought we'd all have breakfast together and discuss that little stunt you pulled last night. Why don't you have a seat?"

"No thanks," I mutter and turn to leave.

The air crackles.

My father explodes from the chair, and the shriek of wood against tile stuns me for the millisecond it takes him to cross the room. He jerks me around to face him. "I don't think you get it," he says in a low voice. "I'm not *asking* you, I'm *telling* you. I've had about enough of this—"

"Let me go." Somehow my voice comes out louder than my thundering heart. "You're not even supposed to be here without another adult present!"

His fingers sink deeper into my skin. "Oh really? Well, then go ahead, Chirp, tell me what else the law says I can and can't do. Come on, you brought it up."

He can't do this. He can't. "Stop it," I croak. My hands spasm, my head bobs. Adrenaline screams fight or flight, but I can't move. Can't choose.

"I am your father," he says and, with his free hand, cups my quavering chin. "I changed your diapers, I taught you how to hit a fastball and how to count and *everything,* and now the state is gonna tell me, now *you're* gonna tell me what I can and can't do? Bullshit." He tugs me up against his chest where the golden baseball blinds my vision and his minty-fresh breath reams my nostrils. "You're my daughter and I love you and nobody's going to stop me from hugging you if that's what I want to do, dammit."

Close the curtain, my mind orders, but the command is small and lost.

His voice cracks. "God, Chirp, how can you be so cold? What happened to that pretty, good-natured little girl with the freckly nose? You used to think I hung the moon, and now . . ."

The air conditioner kicks on and the floor vent blows chilled air up between my trembling legs.

"Are you afraid I'm mad at you for testifying against me? Listen, I don't blame you. You were just a kid, confused and

manipulated, and I wasn't there to protect you. I understand that." He tries to tilt my chin up, to woo my gaze
from his chest to his face.

I don't give.

He sighs. Releases my arm and steps back. "Please don't
make this harder than it has to be. You're still my little girl
and I'm responsible for you, body and soul." His voice
hardens. "You might want to remember that the next time
you decide to break the rules."

He saw me. He *touched* me. If I swallow, I'll throw up.

"Now, why don't you go get dressed before your mother
comes back with breakfast?" He lays strong hands on my
shoulders and turns me in the direction of my bedroom.
"Go ahead, now," he says and whacks me on the butt.

I jolt forward and scurry into my four-sided box.

"And take a shower while you're at it," he calls after me,
sounding vaguely offended. "You smell pretty ripe."

"Okay." I shut the door and pace blind, helpless circles
in the middle of my bedroom. . . .

*I pat bubbles onto my face in a beard. Then lower where a puff of
froth gives me the hair I don't yet have. But I'm getting there because
today I go from being a baby in a bathtub to a big girl who rinses off
under the shower.*

*I grasp the shower curtain and balance on the edge of the tub so I
can see my slick, soapy body in the mirror.*

The bathroom door opens. "Ready for the shower?" my father

56

says, stopping as he catches sight of me. "What the heck are you doing?"

"Getting big," I say, grinning at him through my sudsy beard.

He closes the door behind him. Locks it. "Don't be in such a hurry to grow up, okay? You're perfect the way you are." He is shirtless and the baseball gleams like treasure in his chest hair.

I reach to touch it and slip.

Instantly, his hands cup my armpits. "Careful there." He nudges my nose with his and comes away with a puff of soap clinging to his lip. "Uh-oh, old timer, your beard's falling off! Time to get wet!" He leans into the tub toward the faucet.

"No!" I shriek, laughing and clinging to him like a monkey, wrapping my arms around his neck and my spindly legs around his waist. "Don't drop me, Daddy!"

"Never happen," he promises, pulling me in even closer. . . .

The memory slams me back into myself. I glance around my room, find what I need, and walk to the bathroom. Turn on the exhaust fan and the shower.

I go back out to the hall linen closet, closing the bathroom door behind me to contain the billowing steam, and as I open the closet I call, "Hey Dad, will you make me a fresh pot of coffee, please?" I pause, listening to his silence. Is he suspicious of my sudden capitulation or will his ego chalk it up to a wooing well done?

"Sure," he calls back, sounding pleased. The newspaper pages swish and his chair grates away from the table.

"Thanks!" I dart into my bedroom instead of the bathroom, closing and locking the door, praying his task and the steadily drumming shower will blunt the stealthy sounds I'm about to make.

Because I'm leaving. Not for good, but for now. I need to get a grip and rethink my original plan. Being older and obnoxious isn't going to drive him away and I hadn't counted on my mother disregarding the supervised visit guidelines so quickly. I can't be caught unprepared like this again.

I pull on a fresh tank top and the overalls lying in a crumpled heap where I left them. Stuff my cigarettes into the bib pocket. Grope under my pillow for my pocketknife—a fifteenth birthday gift from Nigel—and wedge it into my front pocket.

I hurry across the room. Raise the blind and grasp the bottom of the window, pressing the metal release clasps. I am about to slide it open when I see my mother's car meandering around the blind curve.

"Crap," I mutter and pull back out of sight. Will she notice the raised, crooked blind breaking the symmetry of all our windows as she approaches the front of the building? Of course she will.

I bite my lip, glance at the bedroom door. The lock is standard and flimsy. Once she parks and comes in, I'll have only seconds to raise the window, bust through the screen, and climb out before she asks my father why my blind is hanging at such an odd angle. Only seconds to bolt in broad daylight from the front of my building to the back of Andy's and get inside. I pray his mother hasn't had milk for breakfast as she's lactose-intolerant and becomes bathroom-bound whenever she dips into dairy.

I spot my watch on the nightstand, crawl across the bed, snag it, and slip it onto my wrist. The knife bangs against my thigh and I realize I'll need it to slice through the screen. I open the blade just as I hear the muffled *thunk* of a car door slamming outside my window.

Her keys jingle.

My heart booms.

The front door opens.

I wrench up the window as the front door closes behind her. My hair swings in front of my eyes and I jam it behind my ears. The scent of fresh coffee fills the air. I plunge the knife into the screen and yank downward, surprised at how little resistance the mesh gives. The slicing makes a harsh, zipping sound.

"Chirp?" my father calls from the kitchen. "Get a move on. The bagels are here and they're still hot."

I jam my leg through the gash, wincing as the rigid frame bruises my groin, and bend myself in two trying to get out. My head collides with the metal frame and stars dance in front of my eyes. I wiggle through the jagged tear, clutch the sash, and drag my other leg through.

"Chirp?" Out in the hallway.

The drop is seven feet and I'm five foot six. The lawn slopes away from the building and I stumble backward as I touch down, then sit hard. I scramble up and cast a panicked glance at ancient, wide-eyed Grandma Calvinetti and one of her twin grandsons sitting on her front porch across from us.

She crosses herself and covers his eyes.

I take off around the blind side of my building, down the lawn in four lightning strides, across the court, behind Andy's building, and up his back steps.

I rap the glass and press up against the door. If my father comes out our back door instead of the front he'll spot me immediately and it'll all be over. Feverishly, I wonder how much time the lock will buy me and know it won't be much. Minutes? Seconds? My father is already suspicious; how long will he wait to break into my room when I don't respond?

The answer comes almost immediately.

"What the . . . ? " His astonished voice floats out of my bedroom window and through the morning air.

"What is it, Charles?" my mother says. "Oh my . . . someone broke in?"

"Not *in,* you idi—" My father stops and then, "Mere-dith? Meredith?"

His voice is much clearer now and I imagine him poking his head out of the torn screen, scanning the area, searching for me.

"Charles, what are you doing?" my mother asks. "I thought you said Meredith was taking a shower. Where are you going?"

"Out to find her," he says, his voice fading.

I shrink closer to the door, hammering again with my knuckles. Come on, Ms. Mues. Come on. Come *on.* I cup my hands around my eyes and peer in through the crack in the curtains. The kitchen is empty.

Of course it is. She's in her room packing for Iowa or in the bathroom imprisoned by cramps or—

A shadow cuts through the kitchen.

I straighten as Ms. Mues shuffles toward the door. Cast a nervous glance over my shoulder.

The curtains twitch apart. She peers out, her nonpre-scription glasses magnifying her perfect 20/20-vision eyes into giant boiled eggs, and her moon face creases in a smile.

"Well, good morning, Mer—" she begins, opening the door.

"Shh," I hiss, plowing straight into her and rudely herd-ing her backward into her own kitchen. I ease the door closed behind me, hearing, as I do, the sharp, angry crack of

61

my front door slamming. "My father's after me." My composure takes a header and I'm caught in a full-body tremor. "He . . . he . . . he . . ."

"Not in here," she says, wrapping her great arm around my quaking shoulders, sweeping me out of the kitchen and away from the windows. "We'll go into Andy's room, honey, and you can tell us both exactly what's going on."

We are halfway down the hallway when the knocking begins.

chapter nine

H e didn't see me come in here, I know he didn't," I babble. "I didn't tell him about you guys, I swear. He must be going door to door."

"I see." Her face pales, but her composure doesn't falter. "Well, I'm not as ready for this as I wanted to be, but with any luck he'll never even know it's me." She nods and squeezes my shoulder. "Don't you worry, honey. I'll take care of it."

"Yes. Okay." I can't stop shivering even though her bulky body and unflappable attitude comforts me in a way I'm just beginning to understand.

Andy and his mother are not "that fat slob Jesus freak and her crippled kid," as my mother so ignorantly calls them whenever she's forced to acknowledge their existence. One of the many things my mother doesn't realize is that Ms. Paula Mues is actually Mrs. Paula Beecher, the same widow my father cheated on her with so many years ago. She doesn't realize it because Paula Beecher was a slim, doe-eyed brunette in blue jeans and T-shirts, a technical engineer who'd done a stint in the army and backpacked the Appalachian Trail.

I've seen Ms. Mues's old pictures, so I know how completely the extra weight, gray-streaked hair, and black-framed magnifying glasses have altered her appearance. Ever since learning about Andy's molestation at my father's hands, Ms. Mues has devoted her life to atoning for the tragedy and somehow smiting her enemy, which is why she changed her looks, went back to her maiden name, and followed us to Cambridge Oaks.

When it comes to my father, Paula Mues and forgiveness have completely parted company.

The knocking continues.

"You go on into Andy's room and don't come out no matter what you hear," she says. "And don't let him come out, either."

"What're you gonna do?" I ask, pawing her arm.

She chooses the largest ceramic Jesus hanging on the wall and reverently removes it. "I've been waiting a long time for Him to reveal His plan to me and now I'll go forth to do His will. I am a soldier in my Lord's Army."

"Wait! What if he recognizes you?" I say in a hoarse whisper.

"He won't," she says, glancing down at herself with a faintly bitter smile. "I'm as good as invisible to him. The bigger I am the more he won't see me, honey. You know how your father is."

Yes I do, which is why I didn't brush my hair or shower for his homecoming. Physical imperfections have always offended him, but apparently my bad hygiene wasn't repellent enough. Perhaps Ms. Mues's full-blown adulthood will be.

Be careful, I want to say, but she's already shuffling back into the kitchen, Jesus cradled in the crook of her arm and a litany of prayer pouring from her lips.

"I'm coming," she calls serenely as the pounding intensifies.

"Mer?" Andy says. "Is that you?"

Oh God. "Shhh!" I whip into his bedroom doorway, collide with his wheelchair, and sink to the floor in a silent howl, rocking and clutching the fast-rising knot on my shin. A half-second later I press a finger to my lips and mouth, *My father!*

Andy pales. He grips his wheels as if to roll forward, but retreats instead.

"Good morning." Ms. Mues's voice goes southern and singsongs back from the kitchen. "How can I help another child of God?"

"Huh? Oh, well, uh, I'm looking for my daughter and I thought maybe you might have seen her," my father says, and stiff distaste flavors his words. "She pitched a fit and took off on me. She's, uh, fifteen, long brown hair, stands about so high . . . ? " Pause. "She lives in the end unit right over there."

At the first sound of my father's voice, Andy jerks as if he's been slapped. Sweat blooms on his forehead. "He used to call me Buddy," he whispers. "Oh, fuck me, I think I'm gonna puke."

I thrust the wastebasket up into his arms and turn away as he heaves into it.

Andy was five when his father died, seven when my father stepped up to the plate and became the new man in his life. For close to a year Andy had an almost-dad to lean against and look up to. But during the last month of my father and Ms. Mues's relationship, Andy began fighting in school, getting in trouble, and wetting his bed. His moods swung from anxious and clingy to sullen and raging, and—

"That little lost lamb of God?" Ms. Mues carols. "Of course I've seen her."

I stiffen and back slowly away from the bedroom doorway.

"I see her on her way to school every morning at seven-thirty when I open my curtains and praise Jesus for giving me another glorious day to sing His praises."

"No, that's not what I—" my father says.

"Poor sweet baby, she trudges along like she carries the weight of the world on her shoulders and I just *know* if she gave herself to Jesus her pain would be lifted. I've offered to save her, but—"

"Okay no, well, I mean, uh, thanks anyway," my father interrupts.

"Wait, don't leave. No one is lost who seeketh the Lord! Tell me, brother, have you been saved?" Ms. Mues's voice rises. "Would you like to pray with me?"

Silence.

Finally, the door closes and the lock snaps shut.

"Works every time," Ms. Mues says, but her voice trembles beneath the triumph. "Thank you, Jesus, for giving me the strength to face my enemy. In your name, amen." She lurches into sight at the head of the hallway, a tactically superior nuclear submarine disguised as a lumbering tugboat. "It's all right now, honey. He's checking next door, but the Eisners are in Bermuda. I think half the building is away on vacation. Come have coffee. I'll close the blinds. We won't have an audience."

I glance at Andy, who sits slumped with the soiled wastebasket cradled in his arms. "You okay?"

"Yeah," he says, rubbing his forehead and avoiding my eyes. "I just . . . I . . . ." He looks smaller, weaker. Fragile. "How can you take it?"

I shake my head.

We sit at the table and I recount the events of the past twenty-four hours.

When I'm done, Ms. Mues sighs and removes her thick glasses. Her eyes shrink back to normal size and bring sad beauty to her face.

"He's an abomination," she says, glancing at Andy, who hasn't spoken yet.

"But a smart one," I say. "He only messes with me when no one else is around. He hasn't reformed, he's just gotten sneakier." I stop, feeling an absurd pang of conscience at my disloyalty. I have every reason to hate him—his betrayal colors all that I am, have been, and will be—but it's hard to shake the lessons learned before the souring, not the least of which is "blood is thicker than water."

Stupid, I know. But there all the same.

"So much for those empathy classes and the psychological evaluation," Ms. Mues says, rubbing her forehead. "And the parole board's not winning any prizes, either. This was a terrible, violent crime. They all were." She glances at Andy, at the bottle wedged between his thighs, and pain sweeps her face. "Why do these people keep getting out? Why aren't they sentenced to life without parole or put in a mental hospital? I don't understand this world. What's the point of obsessing over cholesterol or bike helmets or even cigarettes when the biggest threats to our children are being released back into society every day? Yes, maybe *some* of them have reformed, but what about the ones who haven't? Doesn't anyone realize that one *touch,* one *time* will destroy a child's life ten times faster than a pack-a-day habit?"

It's not really a question, so I don't bother to answer.

Instead, I remember my mother's delight when the call came announcing my father's release date. . . .

"Why, that's wonderful!" she says, cradling the phone and beaming at me across the kitchen. Outside the Calvinetti twins argue over an iPod. "I'll take the day off. Really? Oh, I see." Her expression clouds, then clears again. "No, I'm sure we can work around it. Anything to make this happen. Thank you for calling!"

I stare at my spoon, watch the tomato soup vibrate off it in spurting splashes. It's all right, though; I'm no longer hungry.

She hangs up and laughs with delight. "Your father's coming home early!"

I set the spoon down on my napkin. The puree stains the white tissue. I move the spoon into the bowl and crumple the napkin. It's hard to breathe.

"That was the attorney. He said the doctors are very pleased with your father's progress and that his behavior has been exemplary—"

"Well, that's stupid." My reaction is rude and raw. "Of course he's been a model prisoner, Mom. There aren't any kids to molest in prison."

"There's so much to do to get ready," she says, as if I haven't spoken. "He'll need new clothes and a job, a place to live—"

I straighten. "Not here?"

"Well, no, the attorney says that's one of the rules of his release,"

she says, avoiding my gaze. "He can't live with us just yet. He's on some sort of parole or whatever, with a lot of guidelines. I don't know what they are yet, except . . ." Her face darkens. "He has to register down at the police department because of his . . . situation."

"Good," I say and the rest tumbles out fast and faster. "Because that's exactly what he SHOULD have to do, and you know what? I hope they put his picture online so that everybody will know he's a child molester because that's what he is, Mom, just like all those other gross old guys in chat rooms trying to—"

"Stop it!" She turns on me, fierce. "Don't you ever talk that way about your father! He had a breakdown, do you hear me? He didn't understand what he was doing. We were stressed, I was going to school and working full-time and you know how affectionate your father is, you know how much he loves being the center of attention. He wasn't trying to hurt anyone, he was trying to show you love and maybe get a little in return. He was lonely, Meredith, that's all. Lonely and needy and he made a mistake."

"Is that what you really think?" I say, aghast.

"It's true. It was a mistake."

"Wrong." I lunge forward, white-knuckling the edge of the table. "Rape is not a mistake! He did it on purpose, over and over again because he wanted to, because he got off on it—"

"Meredith!" She cuts me off, furious. "Why do you do that? Why do you always have to make things ugly? If I'm willing to forgive and forget, why can't you? My God, there are thousands of kids out there who'd love to have a father—"

"Well, they can have mine, because I don't want him and I'm not gonna have anything to do with him no matter WHERE he lives." I shove my chair from the table. The tomato soup sloshes out of the bowl and drenches the place mat. "I hate him and I hope he dies!"

She snatches the place mat and runs it to the sink. "Don't ever say that again. He's paid his dues—"

"Three years?" My panic expands. "Mom, people get more jail time for shoplifting! He was supposed to be locked up for nine years so by the time he got out I would have been legal and gone."

"Oh, I see," my mother says with a grim sort of triumph. "You want your father to rot in prison and me to be alone for another six years just so you can have your own way. Well, guess what? The world doesn't always revolve around you."

My head is spinning. "He molested five kids and those are only the ones who got up the nerve to tell. Who knows how many others are out there?"

"This conversation is over," she says, walking away.

I follow her. "How can you even look at him? How can you kiss him? Do you know where his mouth has been?" The nightmares in my brain are roaring.

"Done." Her features are smoothed and straightened. She's re-made herself and anything I say will bounce off her now, the way a quarter bounces off a tight sheet. "Your father and I have been to-gether for twenty-seven years—"

"Yeah, I know, since you were twelve and he was sixteen," I say.

"Didn't you ever think it was weird that a sixteen-year-old guy would want to be with a middle school girl? Doesn't that seem a little sick to you, Mom?"

Dull red stains her face and she looks like she hates me. "No sicker than you always being Daddy's little girl and hogging him all for yourself, so you know what, Meredith? Excuse me if I'm not as sympathetic as you think I should be." Her jaw tightens. "I've always wondered why, if what he was doing to you was so horrible, you didn't tell on him sooner . . ."

Stricken, I put out a hand to stop her. "Mom, I—"

"No, now it's my turn. I hate what happened, and maybe you want to dwell on it for the rest of your life, but I don't. As far as I'm concerned, it's done. If you can forgive and forget, fine. If not, then when you're eighteen, go. We'll survive. We were together before you showed up and we'll be together after you leave. I am not throwing away my marriage just because something that shouldn't have happened did. The best thing to do is get over it and move on." Her face lights up. "And now we can because he's finally coming home!"

It's then I realize that if it comes down to making a choice between my father and me, she will choose him. . . .

I watch Andy's mother, who is watching Andy disappear into himself.

She will choose him.

Oh God, I want so badly to believe that Ms. Mues shelters me because she cares and not because I'm a source of inside information on the enemy. I long to trust her completely, but right now I don't. I hate it when I get like this.

I think I'm skittish partly because she's gone and done the unacceptable, made herself "unattractive and unappealing" just to get close enough to wreak revenge for her son's corruption. In my family, you can rot to hell on the inside as long as you're flawless on the outside, which is really sick, but also hard to unlearn. So while the true and desperate core of me applauds Ms. Mues's selfless sacrifice and adopts some of her methods for my own, the shallow outside that grew up with the Shale credo still shudders at her deliberate lack of grooming, even though we're *both* doing it for a good cause.

"I have to go," I say and stand up because I'm drowning in mixed messages and warring truths. The air in the kitchen is dead and glassy-eyed saviors stare at me from the walls.

I should have a plan and someone to trust, but I don't. I should have taken my vitamins, but I didn't.

Ms. Mues shields me just to thwart my father. She doesn't really care for me. She's a plotter, a planner, and what better way to avenge her son than to destroy her enemy's daughter? To gain my trust and use me to achieve her goal, much like my father used Andy for his own perverted satisfaction.

And how can Andy love a girl whose father wooed a lonely little boy mourning his own dead dad, then moved in to betray him?

I want Andy to love me, but I know now that he can't. If he weren't paralyzed, he wouldn't even be with me. He's nineteen, beautiful, and legal. I'm not. He tolerates me because I am here and available, and I am something to do. I win by default; there is no one else in the race. . . .

We lay twined together in bed, an old Counting Crows CD playing low, the shadows broken only by a thin, gray shaft of listless, winter light slouching in through the window. Moist warmth cools on our bare chests. Andy was hard this time, a rare occurrence, and one he doesn't like mentioned or even noticed, but I couldn't help feeling it pushed against me through his jeans. He's never said why we don't go any further and I've never asked, content just to be with him like this and maybe knowing deep inside that some ghosts are too cruel to question. But now I'm thinking of the four years between us and it worries me. Four is my best number, but there are four years between my parents, too, and I would rather fall down dead than find out we're anything like them.

Twelve and sixteen is much different than fourteen and eighteen, isn't it? Twelve and sixteen is a seventh grader and a high school junior. Fourteen and eighteen could be a freshman and a senior. That's no big deal, it happens all the time. And besides, it's not about numbers with us, it's all about maturity and common interests and love . . . isn't it?

74

"Andy?" I whisper, tracing a pale blue vein up his arm. "If it wasn't me, would it just be someone else?"

"Mmm?" He stirs, tightening his embrace and gazing down at me from beneath sleepy lids. "Sorry, Mer. Did you say something?"

I burrow my face into his shoulder, appalled at what I've almost done. My parents, my father, have no business in this room. "No," I whisper, voice muffled. "I'm fine. . . ."

"Meredith?" Ms. Mues says, cocking her head.

"I have to go," I repeat, backing away from the table.

"Go where? What's wrong?" She plants her palms on the table and heaves up after me. "Honey, what's the matter? Andy, Meredith says she's leaving."

Andy blinks and returns to the land of the living. "Where are you going? I didn't even give you the house keys yet."

"It's okay, I'll come back later," I say, scrabbling behind me for the doorknob. I have to get out of here. Control has left me and if they try to help I will bite.

"Honey, if I said something wrong—" she says, but I slip out and the door closes on her apology.

The glaring sunlight shocks my skin.

My head is pounding. The doubts are winning.

chapter ten

I jog to the far end of Andy's building, press my back against the hot brick, and peer around the side like a cheesy, B-movie spy.

I don't feel cheesy, though. I feel like I'm running for my life.

I cross the court and slip around the adjacent building, crunching over the baked grass and working my way to the front of the complex. I hate being out in the open, but it's the only way to get to the main road.

The Mobile Mechanic truck rumbles past me through the complex, on his way to tune up Ms. Mues's Cadillac for their trip.

The sight of it feeds my panic.

They'll be gone soon, so why had I run from Andy?

Because I hadn't expected him to break down so quickly.

Wrong.

I hadn't expected him to break down at all.

But then again, I hadn't expected him to leave me and trot off to Iowa, either.

I've missed seeing a lot. I will have to look closer.

I skirt a pile of mummified dog crap and keep on going. Sweat beetles down my temples to my neck and disappears into my tank top.

I've been wrong too many times over the past twenty-four hours and it rattles me. My biggest mistake is in believing there are limits to how bad it can get.

I clench the sheet tight under my chin but it's no use.

"Come on, Chirp," my father murmurs, tugging it free and guiding my hand down under the covers. "It's all right."

Shaking, I stop and light a cigarette. Inhale. The smoke burns my throat.

If the victim soul in Iowa cures Andy's paralysis, he'll be able to walk again.

I come home from school to find a raggedy bouquet of daisies on my front porch and wheelchair tracks shortcutting across my lawn. Look over to see Andy smiling from behind his sliding glass door. . . .

Stand upright. Hold me. Screw me.

It's midnight and still snowing. Andy and I have been sitting in the dark in front of his sliding glass door for hours, whispering, laughing, holding hands, and watching the magical flakes swirl and dance in the streetlight's glow. . . .

I walk faster. My mind is reeling.

If you don't count incest, I'm still a virgin.

I don't know if Andy's a virgin. I don't know what he did in the time span between my father and his crippling accident. He doesn't seem like a virgin, though. He knows too much about how and what to touch to be a beginner.

"What are you doing?" I say hoarsely as he trails a finger from the beauty mark on my rib cage to the one on my hip, leaving a path of goose bumps in his wake.

"Connecting the dots," he murmurs with a wicked look. "Uh-oh, you made me lose my place. Now I have to start all over again. . . ."

I've never seen him with his pants off.

My father has. My father's seen both of us.

And it's *wrong,* wrong and unfair that he could have done what he did and be allowed back for more. Wrong that no one will stop him.

I will stop him.

I rage past the front of my father's building, bare feet pounding the pavement, fists ready, daring him to see me, to order me to *stop right there!,* but his blinds are closed and I pass unchallenged.

I don't feel panicky or disloyal anymore. I am David facing Goliath, eager to rework my strategy, fling my killing stone and annihilate the bully.

I scale the hill to the main road and head for my grandmother's.

chapter eleven

My grandmother, Leah Louisa Delklap, lives at the east end of Estertown. The houses are stately, graced with gently rolling lawns and ancient maples. In comparison, our pricey condo complex with its manmade retention pond and weeping cherry saplings is a raw upstart, a blotchy birthmark on the town's otherwise smooth complexion.

It takes me forever to arrive because I follow all the neighborhood back roads. I skirt groups of gossiping adults who fall silent as I pass and I avoid their kids who aren't silent at all, and who do their best to remind me of who I am. They would be happy to know that they've always made it impossible to forget.

I see my mother's BMW cruising Main Street a few times. I fully intend to meet up with her, but not until my grandmother is there to referee.

Hunger makes my head spin. My overalls are sagging from sweat and the legs drag under my bruised heels. I smell ripe and used and this cracks me up, because I am. Insanely, I wish my father were here now to see and smell me and be revolted by my sloppy self.

My mother's car is parked in my grandmother's driveway.

I flick my hair loose and the curtain closes around me. Open my grandmother's front door and step into the cool foyer. "I'm here," I call, bumping the door shut behind me and ambling toward the kitchen, where an indignant "It's about time!" echoes and chairs are pushed from the table.

My grandmother reaches me first. She's wearing crisp, white capris, a sporty Ralph Lauren polo, and sensible sandals. Her short hair is neat and threaded with gray, her gold hoop earrings small and tasteful. Her face is composed but her cheeks are pink and a battle light burns in her eyes.

"Are you all right, Meredith?" she asks, smoothing my sweaty hair from my face with a broad hand so she can get a good look at me.

"I'm hungry." I let her look, mostly because there's no way to stop her.

"Where the hell have you been and what the hell did you think you were doing?" my mother yells. "Do you know how long your father's been out looking for you in this heat? I swear, I don't know what possesses you sometimes!"

"Yes you do," I say flatly.

She snakes a rigid arm around my grandmother and jabs her finger at my nose. "Don't start. I'm warning you."

"Really, Sharon, can't you see you're only making matters worse?" my grandmother says, shifting and forcing my mother to abandon her accusing stance. "Why don't you go pour the iced tea while Meredith showers?"

"Why bother?" my mother says. "She'll only run away again."

"No I won't," I say. "There's no reason to, *here.*"

"I left you alone for *ten minutes*—"

"You weren't supposed to leave me alone at all! There's a reason for that, remember? How long did you really think it would take him to start again?"

My mother goes white. Her mouth opens but no words come out.

"Meredith." My grandmother grips my shoulders. "Are you saying he . . . ?"

I'm tempted to take the convenient shortcut, but DNA tests and rape kits will brand me a liar and then when I really do need help, no one will believe me. "No," I say and grant my mother breath. "But he *could* have."

"You just won't let it go, will you?" my mother snaps and rubs her temple.

"This isn't getting us anywhere." My grandmother steers me toward the stairs. "Meredith, go take a shower. Hand out your clothes and I'll wash them. My robe is hanging on the back of the door. Sharon, go into the kitchen and start lunch." She's using her official mayor's voice now and it's easy to see why even after my father's scandal, she wasn't asked to resign from office.

"I'm not hungry," my mother says as I head upstairs. "I have to find Charles and tell him Meredith's turned up. The poor man must be on the verge of an apoplexy by now."

"Only if he thinks I'm down at the police station reporting him for not registering as a sex offender yet," I toss back without pausing.

"He hasn't registered yet?" my grandmother says grimly.

"He has a couple of days from the time he was released," my mother says. "We'd planned to go down as a family after breakfast, but then Meredith had to pull this stupid stunt—"

"Oh, there's a wholesome outing," I say. "Let's all skip down to the cop shop to register my daddy as a pervert. What fun."

"That's enough," my grandmother says, but it sounds like she agrees with me. "And Charles will survive another twenty minutes without you, Sharon. He can go register alone. Or if you must go with him, call and leave a message telling him to wait another half hour because before you leave, we three are going to sit down and find a workable solution to this problem."

I cross the upper landing and head for the bathroom.

"Now," my grandmother says, "does Meredith still like tuna salad?"

"No," I shout, because my mother doesn't know what I like anymore. "I don't eat things that bleed. Just cheese with lettuce or tomato with mayo. No dead fish or animals, please."

"You see what I have to put up with?" my mother says.

I open my mouth to answer, then think better of it as it will only irk Leah Louisa and I need her on my side.

"She's a teenager," my grandmother says and her voice grows stronger as she mounts the stairs. "Let's focus on the bigger issues, shall we?"

I close the bathroom door and strip down, careful to stow my cigarettes, lighter, and knife in the pocket of my grandmother's robe before I hand my soiled stuff through the cracked door.

"What about your underwear?" she asks, accepting the grubby wad.

"Well, I left in kind of a hurry, Gran," I say, catching sight of myself in the full-length mirror. I'm nasty. Messy. I look like I'm wearing dirt-gray Peds and with a little more knotting and studied neglect I will have perfect Rasta hair.

"All right," she says, sighing. "Come down when you're finished."

My feet ache and there's a purple knot above my eyebrow where I whacked my head climbing out the window. It's tender and I don't press on it again.

The shower is heaven, though, with forty-four perfectly square tiles and four thick guest towels. The blue in the bathroom is pure and pristine, and reminds me of the serene eyes and painted robes of the oak Madonna icon next to Andy's bed.

A victim soul is a pious individual chosen to absorb the suffering of others.

That boy needs a good shrink and some physical therapy, not some corn-fed quack quoting Scriptures and waving a crucifix.

I twist off the water and open the curtain. Grab a towel and blot my skin. Slip into the striped cotton robe, perch on the hamper, switch on the fan, and light a cigarette.

I don't know what to think about this.

Is Andy really suffering in the curable sense? Because he isn't ill, he's paralyzed—and not from birth, either.

He was hanging out an SUV window on the night of his high school graduation, whooping and waving his diploma, one of dozens in a wild, snaking caravan of cars on the way out to party.

Andy's buddy, the driver, had started drinking early. He'd gunned the engine and whipped a right onto Main Street. Cut the corner too short and bounced over the curb. Andy, hanging up to his waist out of the passenger window, had hit the steel stop sign chest-first and the impact flung him out onto the road.

I wedge my cigarette in my mouth and squint against the acrid smoke.

If Andy has no physical pain, then what suffering does Ms. Mues want cured?

I think of the scars knitted across his body and the "accident-prone" label. Of the stories Ms. Mues has told me about Andy's postmolestation childhood.

Crashing bikes into walls. Rollerblading into traffic. Falling off the monkey bars and out of trees. Bungee jumping off the roof with a homemade tether.

I run my cigarette butt under the faucet and hide it in the wastebasket.

Getting high. Driving drunk. Picking fights. Unprotected sex?

The accident, numbing half but not all of him.

I rip a comb through my hair, yanking at knots and making my eyes tear.

Gallons of Jim Beam. Gallons.

Open the bathroom door and emerge in a cloud of smoky steam. It dissipates fast, no match for sunlight and air-conditioning, leaving me chilled and seeing clearly.

Ms. Mues isn't praying for Andy to walk again.

She's praying for him to want to live.

chapter twelve

I belt the wrap robe over the pocket with the cigarettes in it, but I can tell by my grandmother's arched eyebrow that I'm not fooling her.

"Two tomato sandwiches with two pickles," she says instead, setting down the plate and sinking into the chair beside me. "Eat first and then we'll talk."

Four. Good. I devour the pickles first. Yum, salt.

"Oh, come on, Mother," my mother says. "Meredith can talk and eat at the same time." She slumps against the countertop and folds her arms across her chest. "And it's not like I haven't heard all this before. So let's just get it over with so I can take my daughter, go home to my husband, and get on with my life."

I wolf down the first sandwich and am into the second by the time my grandmother answers.

"Well, I guess that's a beginning." Leah Louisa turns to me. "All right, Meredith, you've heard what your mother wants. What do *you* want?"

I want my father gone but I can't say that, so I chew slowly, buying time to readjust my goal. My original plan of making myself repulsive and driving him away isn't working. Staying out of his orbit is going to be impossible with both him and my mother insisting on a harmonious reconciliation.

The tomato sandwich tastes sour now. I don't want to be run out of my own home, but I don't want to live near my father, either. On the other hand, the only thing standing between exile and me *is* my father. He will never let me move away; my mother would send me here to live with Leah Louisa in a heartbeat.

If I were to stay here, I'd be safe, but alone and monitored. Leah Louisa would never put up with my disappearing act, especially if I came in with swollen lips and bed hair, smelling of Jim Beam and Andy. Living here would mean no more purification Fridays, no Nigel and Gilly, no easy access to Andy, and no freedom.

Freedom. Free to do what? Cower and run and hide? Free to be made small and disgusting, to listen to my father's obscene desires, feel his gaze creeping over me, waiting for me to make that *one* wrong move so he can pounce. . . . Who is free? Not me. He's the only one who's free. He's the only one doing exactly what he wants . . .

Oh.

Hope flares, hot and immediate, and I almost drop the sandwich. Of course. It's so simple. When he reoffends, he'll be sent back to prison. Probably for a long time, maybe even forever if his next victim is as messed up as I was and the enraged parents go straight to the police afterward. . . .

If.

Afterward.

Oh no. No, I *can't.*

I don't want to be the sacrificial lamb. I can't go through it again, not unless I'm guaranteed a nick-of-time save and unshakable sanity, neither of which seem available. It's too much to ask of anyone, and yet . . . if I don't stake myself out, sooner or later somebody else, somebody innocent and still pure, is going to get caught in my father's web and it will be my fault for not stopping him.

"Meredith?" Leah Louisa prods.

I blink and am back on the battlefield, scrabbling desperately for another way. "Why do I have to be around him, Mom? You're happy he's back. I'm not. You want time alone with him and I'm *trying* to stay away, but you just keep forcing him down my throat." I pause and my mother's mouth tightens. She thinks I've said it to taunt her, but I haven't. "Why can't you just leave me out of it?"

"Because family sticks together." Her mascara's left raccoon smudges under her eyes and her armpit stubble needs shaving. She won't like what she sees when she gets home and will blame me for causing her sloppy grooming.

"Then why don't *you* stick with *me?*" I ask. "Why don't you tell him that some things aren't forgivable and there's no making nice or starting over—"

"You see?" my mother says bitterly, spreading her hands and glaring at my grandmother as if it's somehow all her fault. "There's no talking to her. She hears what she wants to and that's it. The world revolves around Meredith and nobody else counts."

"Sharon, be reasonable," my grandmother says.

"I'm done being reasonable," my mother says, pushing away from the counter. "I've talked myself hoarse and it's gotten me nowhere. I *know* Charles made mistakes. He's sorry and has promised it'll never happen again, okay? If you think he's stupid enough to get himself sent back there, then you don't know anything at all!" She scowls. "I'm not leaving him, no matter what anybody says. I promised to stand by him for better or for worse, until death did us part. Get it through your heads: *I meant it.*"

The clock over the sink ticks like a bomb.

"So there's nothing he could do that would drive you away," my grandmother says, knotting her hands together on the table.

"No," my mother says without hesitation. "He's my soul mate, I love him and . . . well, as a matter of fact, we're trying to have another baby."

"What?" my grandmother says.

I'm up and out of my chair. "You can't be serious!"

"Of course I am." My mother's eyes are lit with an odd sort of triumph. "Charles has always wanted a big family and what better way to show faith in our marriage than to have another baby? A son would be wonderful, don't you think?"

"Sure, Mom, a son would be perfect," I say. "And convenient, too."

But this time my mother doesn't rise to the bait. Doesn't lose control. Doesn't do anything but smile because she knows she has us and there's nothing we can do about it except pray for sluggish sperm and withered eggs.

I plop back into my chair.

"Have you taken your age into consideration?" my grandmother babbles, clinging to the edge of the table like the house has tilted and she's trying not to fall into the abyss. "A woman your age is in a higher risk category for certain birth defects. . . ." She meets my mother's unperturbed smile and forges on. "It's such a huge, irreversible step, Sharon. What about your career? Are you planning on being a stay-at-home mom this time?"

My mother's laugh curdles my stomach. I realize what she's going to say before she even speaks and I cannot bear to hear it.

"Mother, be serious," she drawls. "Charles and I have already talked about this and since I'm the only one earning a decent salary, he'll stay home with the baby. Meredith can help after school. She's going to be sixteen soon and it's time she learned a little responsibility." She glances at me. "So now you see why it's important to put the past behind us. I wasn't supposed to tell anyone yet, but I didn't know how else to make you understand how strong our commitment is to each other." She slips into the chair across from me, face glowing. "Don't you see? This baby-to-be deserves a whole family—"

Leah Louisa clears her throat. "Aren't you getting a little ahead of yourself? You're not pregnant yet. And, well . . . Charles *just* got out yesterday!"

"You'd be surprised at how much you can accomplish in ten minutes," my mother says and actually giggles. "Talk about absence making the heart grow fonder!"

Someone moans and I'm not surprised to discover it's me.

"Sharon, please," my grandmother says, casting me a pointed glance.

"Relax, Mother," she says, smirking and leaning back in

her chair. "Meredith's a big girl. She knows how babies are made, don't you, Mer?"

I nod, numb and weary. " 'Course I do. Same guy that taught you taught me."

Her hand flashes out and slams into the side of my face.

My head explodes and the kitchen swims in kaleidoscope seas.

"Sharon!" My grandmother jumps up. "Meredith, are you all right?"

I make a strange sound and put my hand to my throbbing face.

Leah Louisa grabs my mother's arm and jerks her to her feet. "That's it. Get out." Her fair, mayoral persona is nothing but a memory.

My mother twists free and stares at her. "All right, stop. I'm sorry."

"Sorry doesn't change what just happened."

"But—" my mother says.

"There are no buts!" My grandmother snatches the dirty plates from the table, whirls, and crashes them down into the sink. A chunk of ceramic bounces up and hits the window. "It's too late and it will be too late *forever.* I'm not going to stand by and watch this happen again because you're too stupid to put an end to it!"

I stop breathing.

Incredibly, my mother holds her ground. "Oh, like you ended it when you caught Daddy cheating on you with Mrs. Burt? Funny, I don't seem to remember *you* guys getting a divorce."

My grandmother goes ashen.

"What, you thought it was a secret?" My mother laughs again, uglier this time. "Sorry, Mom, nothing in this neighborhood was a secret. Every kid on the block knew what was going on, me included. Hell, I knew before *you* did."

My grandmother falls back a step, staring at my mother as if she's never seen her before. Seconds pass and when she finally speaks, her words start out shaky but quickly gain strength. "You need to leave now or I'll call the police and have you arrested. We'll see how quickly Charles pawns *his* late father's jewelry to pay *your* bail. Or maybe he won't. Maybe it'd be more convenient to have you out of the way so he can—"

"Stop it!" I shout, caught up in a full-body tremble.

Both women turn in surprise, like they've forgotten I'm even here. My presence abruptly ends the battle.

My mother gives my grandmother one last foul look and heads for the foyer. "Supper at six, Meredith," she tosses back and slams the front door.

The washer buzzes in the background, signaling the end of a load. Robotlike, my grandmother turns and walks out of the kitchen to the laundry room. The dryer starts. The clasps on my overalls clank and clatter, rude in the throbbing silence.

I sit frozen, staring down at the last bite of sandwich. My face feels huge, and a dark weight crushes the center of my brain. My own grandfather . . . and my grandmother had stayed with him. I can hardly stand being in my own family anymore.

Leah Louisa returns, stiff as a sentry, and gazes at the broken dishes as if she can't quite make sense of them. "It wasn't the same thing at all," she says. "Hazel Burt had the morals of an alley cat, and don't think her poor husband didn't know it. Your grandfather was just one of the many fools who fell into her net." She clears her throat and tries again. "Things were different back then. Respectable people didn't air their dirty laundry for the world to see like they do now. Things like that were swept under the rug and the less said, the better. I did what I thought best, given the circumstances. If it happened again today . . ." She shakes her head, lips tight. "I can't prevent your mother from throwing her life away, but I'll be damned if I'll just sit back and let her throw yours away, too."

The declaration is powerful and on some level welcome, but it comes too late. I'd always thought of Leah Louisa as the strong one, the one who spoke her mind and stood up for what was right, the one who never settled or sold out. I'd run to her believing that if she said this mess was over then it would be over, but now I can't unknow what I know and my faith in her is weakened. "How are you going to stop him?"

She summons a grim smile. "You'll move in here with me. He wouldn't dare try anything while you're under *my* roof." She strides across the room, authority in motion, and snatches up a pad and pen. "We have a lot to accomplish and it must be done correctly." She paces, stops, and jots something on the page. "Darn it. Norman always leaves early on Saturday for the lake. I'll have to see him on Monday."

"Who's Norman?" I ask because it seems to matter.

"The family court judge," she says absently, scribbling. "I have to call my attorney, my secretary. . . . Oh, I have a meeting I can't postpone on Monday." She frowns and taps the pen on the paper. "Well, we'll just have to schedule around it."

She makes it sound so simple, so matter-of-fact, like with her taking charge my survival is assured. I can't let myself believe it, and yet there's no stopping me from craving more, from wanting to offer her *all* my dragons. "My father won't let me go."

She snorts and peers at me over the top of her glasses. "Your *father* will have no choice. By the time we're done with him, he'll be lucky if he ends up with an occasional supervised visit, and if I thought I could block those, too, rest assured I would."

I try to hold back, but her words are more potent than vitamins and I sit, blood thrumming, knowing it can't be this easy, and yet . . . "Which room do I get?"

"The blue or the rose, your choice," she says, writing again. "The mattress in the blue room is new, but the view from the rose room is better."

"What about my stuff? My clothes and all, I mean?"

She glances up with a quick frown, like I tripped her in the middle of a full-out stride. "We'll get to that at some point. I don't want you going near that complex by yourself. Now, I need to make some important calls, so why don't you go up and choose a room?"

"Okay." I push back my chair and stand, awkward, wanting to let her know that I'm trying to believe, but all that comes out is, "Which one would you take?"

"The one with the new mattress," she says, picking up the phone. "A good sleep makes all things possible." She studies my face and she sees something, maybe everything I can't say, because she replaces the receiver, crosses the room, and folds me into a fierce hug. "I'm so sorry," she whispers. "I should have forced the issue and done something sooner."

Two people, four arms. Strong numbers. "What could

you have done, Gran? Kidnap me? I mean, up until yesterday everything was fine. If he hadn't gotten out early, none of this would be happening."

"Well, now it is, so let's get busy and solve this problem once and for all." She releases me with a brisk smile and goes back to the phone.

I gather her bathrobe around me and trot upstairs. The bedrooms are beautiful, guest rooms out of a magazine, with polished wood floors and thick throw rugs, matching sheets and comforters, and tons of fringed pillows. The walls have framed old-fashioned paintings on them, one with rich, blue hydrangea bushes and one with lush pink roses. The women in both pictures are wearing long, flowing dresses and have kittens romping at their feet.

I perch on the bed in the blue room, careful not to crease the comforter, and then do the same in the rose room. My cigarettes and knife thud against my thigh as I cross and re-cross the hall. I can't tell the difference in mattresses. The door locks are the same, press-in buttons and flimsy like home. The rose room looks out over Gran's flower garden, the blue room over the quiet street, but neither has a tree branch or a drainpipe near enough to use if I ever need an escape route.

"Meredith?" Gran's voice echoes up the stairs.

I trot out to the landing. "What?"

"I've spoken with my assistant and he's going to meet

me down at my office to work on our strategy and set things up for Monday. We're going to try and reach my attorney, too, so I may be gone for a couple of hours." Pause. "Do you want to come with me or will you be all right here alone?"

I feel my cigarettes nudging my leg. "No, you go ahead. I'll be okay."

"Are you sure?" she asks.

"Just lock the door and I'll be fine," I call back.

"All right, then, I'm on my way." Keys jingle. "I left the direct phone line to my office on the pad by the phone. The TV remote is on the coffee table in the den. I'm taking my laptop with me, but you're free to read any of the books or use the other computer if you'd like. When I get back, we'll order Chinese for supper. How would that be?"

"Fine," I say and wave as she bustles out the door. I listen for the lock's click, then zoom down the steps and double-check it. I remember the back door and race through the kitchen, narrowly missing a stray shard of ceramic plate on the floor, and check that door, too. It's locked and so is the sliding glass. I dart from room to room, checking all the windows, hunkering down to stay below the sills until the last moment so if my father is out there watching the house, he won't be able to follow my progress.

I scurry back up the stairs to the blue bathroom, turn on the fan, and shut the door. Crack the tiny window and light a cigarette. Perch on the cold, hard edge of the tub and use the toilet as an ashtray. It's not the most satisfying way to smoke, nothing at all like hanging out at Andy's. . . .

Andy.

He's leaving for Iowa tomorrow and I never kissed him good-bye. Never even *said* good-bye, just ran out of there like some kind of paranoid lunatic. He doesn't even know I'm safe at Leah Louisa's. No one does.

I should call and tell him, but I can't leave the room with my cigarette. I wish I still had a cellphone, but my mother took it back after my friend Azzah and her family moved to Miami and I'd racked up a six-hundred-dollar bill calling her.

Funny, how bad I'd missed her until Andy moved in and then it was like I'd almost forgotten she'd existed. She forgot me, too, I guess, as she never returned my last call.

I take one last drag, drop the cigarette in the toilet, and flush. Tighten the sash on Gran's robe, crack the door, and slither out, closing it behind me so the smell won't taint the rest of the house. I hate the thought, but I have a feeling my smoking days are numbered. I hurry down to the kitchen and lift the receiver, punch out half of Andy's number, and then stop.

I don't want to say good-bye to Andy over the phone. I need to see him, and I need him to see *me*. I need to be fixed solid in his arms and his mind, not as the one who'd led the nightmare straight to his door this morning, and then freaked and bolted, but as me, Meredith, something good enough to sustain him to Iowa and back. Leaving him with that last awful memory, saying "See ya" over the phone, or sneaking him a covert wave as Leah Louisa and I move my stuff out of my condo isn't going to do it.

I can lose a lot, but I can't lose Andy.

I replace the receiver and scribble my grandmother a note saying I'll be back. I have no key so chances are she's going to come home and find me sitting on her doorstep waiting for her anyway, but still.

My overalls and tank top are almost dry. I change, transferring my stuff from pocket to pocket. I hang my grandmother's bathrobe on a hook and, tucking my hair back behind my ears, slip out through the mudroom door and into the sunlight.

chapter thirteen

I take the direct route back and within fifteen minutes am turning off Main Street into the complex. My overalls are wrinkled but dry from the hot, whooshing breeze stirred by passing motorists.

"FFWHEEEEEEEEEEEEPPP!"

I wince, pause, and track the shrill whistle.

Nigel Balthazar is on his front stoop. "Finally. Come here." His face is florid and the pits of his shirt are dark with sweat. "Christ, don't make me yell. It'll kill me."

I hesitate, then pad up his front walk. I can spare a couple of minutes. "What?"

Gilly appears in the smeary living room window and barks to join us.

"Have a seat," he says, waving me toward one of the two rusty, nylon-strapped lawn chairs squatting in the sun. "I want to show you something."

"You must be kidding," I say, eyeing the spiderweb shrouds draping the chair legs and the bug corpses dangling from the arms, wafting and bumping lazily in the breeze like macabre wind chimes. "What did you do, steal these out of Stephen King's cellar?"

"They're the best I could do on short notice," he says crankily, maneuvering his bulk in front of a chair. He grips the plastic armrests and gingerly lowers himself until the chair stops screeching in protest. His butt scrapes the ground and I have no idea how he will ever get up. "Are you gonna plant it or what?"

I sigh and settle into my hellish throne. Light a cigarette and lay the pack on the rickety table next to a mummified daddy longlegs. My throat is parched and the cigarette makes me cough. "Water?" I look around for a hose.

He frowns at my staccato hack. "You should have said something before I wedged my ass into this torture device. Go into the fridge and grab a couple of Snapples. And you might as well bring Gilly out, too. Her leash is by the door."

"You sure?" I rasp, because I've never been in his condo before.

"Of course I'm sure," he says, deliberately misunderstanding my question. "I just dropped it there ten minutes ago. I may be a relic, but I'm not senile yet, kid."

"A matter of opinion," I say, earning a dark look.

Gilly prances as I make my way through the shabby living room to the kitchen. The place smells of coffee, cigarettes, and dog. Framed police commendations are mounted on the wall around an autographed black-and-white glossy of some leather-faced cowboy actor. It's really old, so it might be John Wayne. Or maybe Clint Eastwood.

Fuzzy white hairballs stir and drift along the hardwood floor as I pass through the doorway separating the living room from the kitchen. There are twelve more pictures hanging here, all scrawled with signatures, all black and white.

"Nigel Balthazar, autograph hound," I murmur, grinning. "Who would've thunk it?" I open the fridge and choose a Snapple grape and a raspberry iced tea. Bump the fridge closed, find Gilly's leash, and lead her back outside.

"Nothing like taking your time," Nigel says. "What were you doing in there, sightseeing?"

"I was star struck," I retort, holding out both Snapples. He picks the raspberry iced tea. Good. I want the grape.

He slams the bottle's bottom against of the heel of his hand, breaking the internal suction, then twists off the cap with a muted pop. Taps it against the cardboard box settled on his lap. "I've been thinking about what you said the other night, how your father's already started harassing you and all."

I open my mouth to say, *Well, guess what? I don't have to worry about that anymore,* but something in his face stops me and sends my stomach into a familiar, downward spiral. "And?" I retrieve my cigarette and open my drink.

"And I don't like it."

"Join the club." A yellow jacket circles my Snapple and I blow smoke rings at it until it flies off in disgust. I may die of cancer, but I haven't been stung in years.

"I'll do better than that," he says and sets the box on my lap. "Open it, but be careful. I had to call in a lot of favors to get my hands on this stuff."

I put my bottle on the table and wipe my damp hands on my overalls. I sit up straighter and carefully open the box flaps. Look at the contents, then at Nigel. "A teddy bear and a smoke alarm? I don't get it."

"Look closer," he says.

The bear is brown, fuzzy, and has glassy black eyes. The cheap, white plastic smoke alarm is the same kind that hangs on my kitchen ceiling. "So?"

"So," Nigel says, "haven't you ever heard of a nanny cam?"

"Yeah," I say and then my eyes widen. "Are these . . . ?"

"Yup," he says, knuckle rapping a cigarette from his pack and wedging it into the corner of his mouth. He lights it and exhales. "We're gonna do us a little covert surveillance, kid. Start building you a case so when the sh— er, crap hits the fan. . . ."

I want to say, *Sorry, but that's not my problem anymore because you see, I'm going to live at Leah Louisa's now,* but the words won't come. I run a finger over the teddy's

108

rounded stomach. "So you think something bad is gonna happen."

"Don't you?"

I shrug and keep my gaze on the bear.

"I know it sucks, but the problem is that we can't do anything until *he* does something. No kid in town, including you, is gonna be safe until he's back behind bars where he belongs." Nigel shakes his head. "He's not one of those guys who wants to change. I wish he was. He's gonna start again, Meredith. It's not *if*, it's *who* and *when* and *how many*."

"I know," I whisper because he's right, it's true, it's everywhere in the heavy, choking air over this complex, but I still don't want to be hung back on the meat hook and sent to the chopping block.

In a better world, I think I would have chosen the rose room.

He drags on the cigarette until the end glows and blows out a thick stream of smoke. "His being alone with you and all? We could probably grab him for a parole violation, but even if he's sent back for it, he's just gonna get out again. We're nickel-and-diming our way through it, you see? But *this* way . . ." He pokes the bear. "Juries love video proof. Bingo-bango, conviction. Makes their job easy."

Conviction. The second sweetest word in the world. I look at the teddy and the smoke alarm, my two new best friends. "What should I do with them?"

"Put 'em wherever it's most dangerous. Each one has a pocket-size remote that'll turn on the camera up to a hundred feet away." He shows me how to work the remotes. "Run them every time you two are in the same room. We'll nail him yet. Think you can do it?"

"Yeah." Despair cracks my voice. "I just don't want to do anything wrong."

His wrinkles deepen and for a second I get the crazy idea that he's near tears.

"You're fifteen years old, kid," he says gruffly. "He's the adult. It's all on him." Clears his throat. "Did I tell you he and I had a little chat this morning?"

"No," I say, closing the box. Four flaps, all interlocking. I move slowly because I'm back on familiar ground and there's no hurry now. "How did that happen?"

He leans back in his chair. "I was sitting here reading the paper when I notice some mope jogging around the complex. And there's something about the way he's moving that makes me wonder what he's doing."

"He was looking for me. We had a situation and I christened that knife you gave me. No, I didn't stab him," I add at his interested look. "I cut through my window screen and took off. Why, what happened?"

"Well, something about him doesn't look right so I figure it's time to do a little investigating, and just my luck, Gilly decides she wants to go for a walk."

110

"How convenient," I say dryly.

"Wasn't it?" His eyes gleam. "So we head down the sidewalk and this guy's jogging past Andy's building, then back to your building, then to the one across from you, and around and around he goes."

"Did you know who he was by then?" I'm fairly sure of the answer.

His mouth thins. "Yeah, I recognized that pointy head right off. Do you know what he had on? His old Estertown Middle School tank. Guy's got nerve."

"You're telling me." My father used to wear that shirt teaching gym class. The only other thing he could wear out in public that would increase the attendance of his lynch mob would be his Boys' League Coach T-shirt, and the way things are going I fully expect to see him wearing it tomorrow.

"So anyhow, I'm just standing there watching him, and he spots me and starts jogging toward me." His mouth slides into a faint grin. "We're oh, maybe fifteen yards apart, and he yells, 'Hey buddy, have you seen my daughter?' and just like that," he snaps his fingers, "he recognizes me. Slams on the brakes so hard he leaves a skid mark. Took off a good chunk of knee, too."

"He fell down?" I can't keep the delight from my voice.

"Made your day, did I?" Nigel says, amused. "So I say,

111

'How you doing, Chuckie? Been a while, huh?' and my tone is nothing but pleasant—"

"He *hates* that name!"

"You don't say," Nigel says and grins. "He gets all defensive and starts in with that 'I haven't done nothing wrong and you cops have no right to stalk me,' sh— er, crap. I wait till he's done ranting and say, 'Been down to register as a chicken hawk yet, Chuck?' Because of course I know that he hasn't. And while he's turning green, I follow up with, 'So Meredith's missing? How'd that happen?' I'm asking because now I'm thinking maybe you two got into it and he's putting on a big show for the neighbors like he don't know you're dead and laying in the Dumpster." He crushes the smoldering butt under his heel. "Sorry to say it, but it happens."

My smile dies. "Yeah, I know." My father can be charming, funny, a caring, good-natured guy always ready to help, a friend to the friendless and a sympathetic ear to kids in need. It's the perfect public persona, and the shock waves after his arrest, the neighbors' absolute denial and disbelief, were a real testament to his acting skills.

Gilly flops over in front of us, panting.

I swirl my Snapple. "So what'd he say when you asked about me?"

"Oh, he got up on his high horse and said, 'I don't have to talk to you! You poisoned my daughter against me,' and I said, 'Didn't have to, Chuck. You did that yourself when you . . . ' " He stops, looking embarrassed.

"Never mind, I get the idea," I say, studying my stubby fingernails.

He shifts and the chair moans in protest. "Well, make a long story short, he takes off for your place and I'm just about to call in the boys on the force to do a Dumpster check, when I see you coming out of Andy's and heading for the road."

"I didn't see you," I say.

"I know. I couldn't yell without drawing your father's attention so I just let you go." Nigel leans over, exhaling a grunt, and pets Gilly, sprawled at his feet. "Now I'm thinking maybe I was wrong. Maybe it'd be good for your old man to know you got friends around looking out for you."

That's the nicest thing anyone's ever said to me. "So that's why we're sitting out here advertising our unholy union."

"Yup." He sits up red-faced. "Think of it as a show of strength."

I fumble for his hand and press it to my cheek.

Nigel clears his throat. "I say something right for a change?"

I nod and release him. "Don't lose any sleep over it, though." I drain the now-warm grape drink, tuck the box under my arm, and rise. "Andy and his mom leave for Iowa tomorrow."

Nigel grips the chair arms, rocking and making the joints scream until he gains enough momentum to lurch to his feet. The chair is crooked and sagging, pitiful in its death throes. "You don't want him to go."

I shrug. "Maybe I'm just jealous that he can." I look away, blinking hard, because *I* could have run. I still can as long as I never look back, never think about my father prowling the complex for other innocent little kids who don't know who he is or what he's going to do to them. I could run back to Leah Louisa's, but I realize now that even if I do there will have to be better locks on the doors, blinds on the windows, and a fence around the yard because I will never be free as long as he's out there, watching and waiting for me.

"Hey kid, listen. You think Andy's running is really gonna solve anything?"

"*He* thinks it will," I mutter and meet Nigel's steady gaze. "Do you?"

"It doesn't matter what I think," he says finally. "Andy's demons chase him just as hard as yours chase you. The only difference is that instead of running, you met yours head-on and that's pretty damn gutsy, considering." He hesitates as if struggling with something and sighs. "That accident where he broke his back? Well, according to the doc, Andy wasn't supposed to be crippled, he was supposed to be able to get up and walk again, but he never did."

I stare at him, knowing I should be more surprised, but instead a dull, steady ache begins at my temples. "Does Andy know? That he should be able to walk, I mean?"

"Yeah, he knows, but you see, it don't matter," Nigel says, toying with his lighter and gazing absently at my father's building. "He's as paralyzed now as he was the minute it happened." He shrugs. "You do what you have to do to survive, I guess. You know that better than anybody and what I think of it doesn't amount to a hill of beans."

It does to me, but I don't say so, as the effort is suddenly too much. I shift the box under my arm. "I should get going."

He shoves his hands deep into his pockets. "Look, your parents went out right before you showed up. You might want to get those cameras installed while they're gone. Practice a little." He hands me a battered business card from when he was on the force. "My home and cellphone numbers are there, but if something happens and you can't get me, buzz 911 and get a cop out here ASAP."

"I hope I don't have to." My stomach is jittering again. "But thanks anyway."

"Don't mention it," he says. I look both ways, then step down onto the hot macadam and plod across the road.

chapter fourteen

The closer I get to home, the harder it is to keep moving forward. I think of Nigel reaching out and Leah Louisa closing ranks, of Andy, whose paralysis runs way deeper than the physical, and of his mother, who craves revenge but is waiting for God to sponsor it.

I think of my father and sunny summer afternoons at the park, of playing catch with a battered old baseball we'd found and later dissected together, taking turns ripping out the stitches holding the worn cowhide closed, unraveling the prickly wool and flattened twine beneath until the hard, dark core was finally revealed. I'd gazed at the unremarkable sphere, hugely disillusioned, and said, *"That's it? That's all it is?"*

"Well, yeah," my father says, looking amused. *"What were you expecting?"*

"Something better," I say, and throw it away . . .

Tires crunch and a car passes.

My head jerks up and my eyes refocus, almost as if I've been asleep. Frantic, I survey the complex, but nothing else stirs. Oh my God, what am I doing? Forget the heat and the weight of the box. I need to get *moving*.

My mother's car is gone so I bullet in the front door and lock it behind me. Pause, listen to the silence, gauge its weight, sniff the air, and decide I'm alone.

I take the box into my bedroom. Set the teddy on the corner shelf next to my stereo, propped up so the doorway and bed are in full view of the camera. Remove the remotes. Press the bear's control. Green light on. Shut it off again.

My heart flutters. Halfway there.

I put the smoke alarm remote in my left pocket and the bear's in my right. Take the alarm cam into the kitchen. Peek out the window into the court. Still deserted.

I can hear myself breathing.

Drag a stool over to beneath the smoke alarm on the ceiling. Lock my fingers around the plastic sides and pull, but it won't come down. Brush my hair from my eyes. My hand comes away wet. How can I be sweating with the air so cold? "Come on." I pry off the cover and spot the screws holding the back plate to the ceiling. Oh God, do we even have a screwdriver?

A car door slams outside. I scramble off the stool and

peek through the blinds. It's only the Calvinettis across the court. I rip through the junk drawer for the screwdriver.

I'm shaking so bad I almost fall off the stool.

I take a deep breath and count off in fours. Four plus four is eight. Four plus eight is twelve. Four plus twelve is sixteen. And so on.

My tremors fade. I replace the old alarm with the cam. "I'm building a case," I say, and the four words become mantra.

It steadies me now but it won't forever. I've done my homework, read books, websites, and message boards, lurked on lists, and even questioned a social worker too exhausted to guard her words, and I know how bad the odds are for girls like me.

We wait to be rescued, but for whatever reason, no one comes. We figure that if no one protects us then we must not be worth protecting so we become prey and are easily picked off. Our wounded, kicked-puppy gazes attract sly predators and we sell ourselves for clearance sale prices, mistaking screwing for caring.

We binge, purge, sleep around. We drink too much and get too high, anything to blot out the past. We accept and endure beatings and humiliations because our fathers, our uncles, and our mothers' twisted boyfriends said they loved us, too, right before they broke our bones and tore our tissue, right before they made us receive them.

I tighten the first screw. Oh yes, I have done my homework.

We have babies because we want them to love us, to make us important, but they only make us tired and fat and stinking of spit up because they're *babies,* not saviors. Their fathers leave us, sick of crap and sour milk, sweatpants and tears.

But the babies still need all of us, only there isn't anything left to give because we based our worth on the lowlifes who knocked us up and around.

So our babies end up screwed up and screwed with because now we're single again, too, so we're bringing home guys who secretly like pink satin baby skin more than our silvery stretch marks. We don't see what we should see because having *anyone* is still supposedly better than being alone.

I know the grim probability of my own future.

The odds are high that the best of me has already been ripped away and that if I don't keep hold of myself I will lose what's left. Without the structure of my rules and rituals, I'm a free-for-all open to any guy who wants to hurt me.

And I don't want to be hurt anymore. I want to be someone who makes it through.

I tighten the final screw. Test the remote.

Put everything away. Slide the cardboard box under my bed.

I'm sorry, Gran, but it has to be this way.

I leave a message on her machine in case she misses the note, saying I had to come home again and that I'll call her soon. Then I head over to Andy's.

chapter fifteen

The Mobile Mechanic's truck is parked next to Ms. Mues's car and the repair guy is leaning into the Caddie's engine. He straightens and looks at me. "Hi."

"Hi," I say, flustered. It's been a long time since someone close to my age has been civil. I clear my throat and nod at the car. "Uh, think it'll make it to Iowa?"

He shrugs. "She runs okay, but the tires show some wear. I don't know if I'd chance it. Kind of a wing-and-a-prayer–type thing."

"Yeah, that'd be about right," I say and head for Andy's.

"You going to Iowa?" he says.

I stop and look at him. Tall, skinny, damp blond hair curling out from under a red bandanna. Curious smile. "Not me. My . . . them." I point to the Mueses' door and see Andy watching from behind the glass. "Well, I better get going."

"Hey." He waits until I turn back to him. "What's your name, anyway?"

"Meredith," I say finally.

He leans a hip against the side of the car. "You live around here?"

I nod cautiously.

"You always so suspicious?"

I nod again.

"Okay." His eyes dance with amusement. "So Meredith, you got a boyfriend?"

The only word I can manage is, "Why?"

He laughs. "Why? Because maybe I want to ask you out sometime."

"Meredith?"

I whirl, spell broken, and see Andy's head poke out the back door.

"Are you coming in or what?" he asks.

"Yeah." My voice is scratchy. I clear my throat. "Yeah." Look back at the Mobile Mechanic who watches me, eyebrow quirked. "I . . . see you." I head for the steps, heart pounding.

"Give me a call sometime," the mechanic says. "You know where to find me."

I wave without turning and slip past Andy's wheelchair into the cool kitchen.

"What was that all about?" he says, closing the door.

"That? Nothing. Oh, he says your car will probably make it to Iowa." I grab a glass and fill it with water. Why do

I feel guilty? I didn't do anything. He's the one keeping secrets.

"Oh yeah? What else did he say?"

I hear something new in Andy's voice.

"He hit on you, didn't he?" he continues, rolling up alongside of me.

"I guess," I say as if it isn't a miracle.

He hoists his bottle, hesitates, and wedges it back between his thighs. "Did you tell him you already had a boyfriend?"

No. Almost. I was going to, but it happened so fast. . . . I glance at his legs, still as stones and thinner than when he'd first moved in. "What if the victim soul cures you?" I say instead. "What's gonna happen when you can walk again?"

"What do you mean?" He hooks a finger into my side pocket and tugs me closer. Slides an arm up around my waist and tries to pull me down onto his lap.

I ease free and wander over to the table. Run my finger along a spent incense stick and tap the long ash into the tray. "You know what I mean. You'll get a job and a car and a real life and then what?"

"Then I have a job and a car and we can go places and do things like normal people." He uncaps the bottle and drinks. Coughs and rubs his eyes. "I don't know what you're getting at, Mer. Don't you want me to walk again?"

In a perfect world, yes, and I'd be there to stand with

him, dance with him, lay down with him. In this world, no, because if he can walk then he'll walk away. "It's not that, it's just that you're putting all your faith into this victim soul person instead of . . . I don't know, other things . . . and I'm just afraid you're going to be disappointed."

"Are you?" he says. "Because it doesn't sound that way at all."

I stare at the table.

"Well," he says finally, flicking back a strand of hair. "I'd better get packing. We're leaving early tomorrow." He rolls his chair forward and back a few times, the equivalent of tapping his foot with impatience.

"I won't keep you then." I put my glass in the sink. "'Bye."

He touches my arm. "Come on, Meredith. I have to do this."

"I know." My voice is distant. "I'm not stopping you."

"Yeah, you are." He rolls in front of me, forcing me to look at him. "Now I have to leave knowing you're pissed at me and Mr. Mechanic's right out there waiting for you."

"What does this have to do with *him*?"

"He can walk, Mer. How am I supposed to compete with that?"

Oh God, he has this all wrong. "I'm not asking you to compete. I don't *want* you to. I just want everything to stay the way it is."

"Yeah, well, it can't." He backs up and wheels around me.

"Andy."

"Look, when I get back I'll walk over and knock on your door," he says with a crooked smile. "Then we can start all over again. How does that sound?"

I push the fluttery panic away. Lean down and rest my forehead against his. "It sounds good." I kiss him and run out before he can see the lie in my eyes.

Down to the sidewalk. Past the Mobile Mechanic, who's on a cellphone, and keep right on going. Step off the curb into the court—

My back door opens and my father struggles out, carrying bags of garbage.

There's no way to duck out of sight.

He looks over at the Dumpster and right at me. "Meredith."

"What?" Amazingly, my voice comes out sullen with no ripples of fear.

He opens his mouth. Looks at the mechanic and at me. "Meredith, come here, please." His tone is deceptively pleasant. "I'd like to talk to you."

Yeah, I bet he would, seeing as how our last conversation sent me diving out the window to escape. "So talk. I can hear you fine from here."

He holds my gaze, but I don't move, and he finally

breaks the stand-off. "Have it your way, then, but I could use a little help," he says, limping down the steps and lugging the garbage toward the Dumpster. The bags are unwieldy, banging against his legs, with the white gauze covering one knee. . . .

I scurry around scooping up Barbie stuff, cramming both hands full, using every single finger because he's promised that if I clean up my mess before the second hand sweeps the twelve, we'll go for ice cream. Breathless, I race to the carrying case, but the lid is shut. I try to flip it open with my bare foot but the catch is locked. "Daddy!" I cry, as the second hand ticks closer to the twelve. I've cleaned up my mess but I'm still going to lose. "Help me! I can't do it by myself!"

Laughing gently, he bends and flips open the case. "Easy, it's not the end of the world. Next time make sure everything's ready to go before you start, okay?"

"Okay." I quickly cram Barbie and her belongings away. Peer at the clock and wilt. The second hand is past the twelve. I didn't make it. I lose.

"C'mon, silly girl," he says, tugging me to my feet. "This was a learning lesson. I figure that's still good for one scoop, right?"

"Right!" My eyes magically dry and my heart swells with love. I hug him because he helped me and one scoop is still better than nothing. . . .

The ache starts in my chest and spreads through my veins. The abuse I can handle; it's the happiness that cripples me.

I go over and pluck a bag from his grasp. "There. Open it."

"Thanks," my father says as if determined to be pleasant. "Looks like they spiffed this thing up recently. Nice paint job." He lifts the lid and heaves his bag up over the side. "Whew, it still stinks, though." Tosses my bag in, too, and lowers the lid. "I looked for you, you know. Ran around like an idiot until I got your mother's message. Are you going to put me through that again or are we gonna go in and talk like normal human beings?"

"Why do I have to go in? It's summer and it's Saturday."

He turns his back on the mechanic and says quietly, "Well, did you ever think that it's been years and I might want to spend some time with you?" His golden baseball catches the sun and flashes like a lighthouse warning of treacherous reefs below.

I wonder if Andy's watching us. I wonder if the mechanic can hear this.

"I've missed you," my father continues. "I'd lay there at night remembering how great we were together, wondering what it would be like if it was just the two of us, if it was *you* I was coming home to. Did you ever think about that, Chirp?"

No, I have never thought about that. Never, on purpose.

"You know what I wish?" he says, stroking the bangs from my forehead.

I lie dead beneath his hands. I am shrunken and shriveled inside, a rotten chestnut hidden beneath a deceptively smooth shell.

"I wish we could make it just you and me," he says. "No one but us. I don't love anybody in the whole world as much as I love you. Maybe someday. . . ."

A door slams behind me and the sound of the Calvinetti twins' squabbling echoes across the court. They're fighting over a soccer ball and don't see us. I watch, stomach sinking, as my father discovers them. Close my eyes and want to scream at the boys for being stupid enough to be seen. They know what he is and what he'll do. Why didn't they just go out their patio door and play in the backyard, safely out of sight? Why are they out here sweating and galloping around right in front of us? Can't they smell his desire? Can't they feel—

"No," I blurt to squash my rising panic.

My father looks back at me, startled. "What?"

I shake my head, too miserable to speak. I know now that I'm the only one who really understands the threat and if I'm ever going to be free of him, really free, once and for all, then I will have to bite the bullet and spend time in his company. Stake out the sacrificial lamb. Uncoil the rope so he can hang himself.

"Anyway." He touches my hand. "There's so much I have to tell you. I was going to keep a journal, but you know how lousy my chicken scratch is. Well, that and I couldn't risk anybody else seeing it. That's why all my letters were so lame. Can't be too careful, right?" His laugh is bitter. "Besides, I'd much rather talk in person. What do you say?"

He's manipulating me and I have to let him. What comes next will be ugly.

In his mind, I am the pure, sweet milk and honey of the Promised Land.

In mine, he's the pointy-toothed cannibal turning the spit at hell's barbecue.

But I have what he wants, and when he reaches for it . . .

I step around him. "Coming?" I toss over my shoulder, heading for home.

chapter sixteen

I go in ahead of my father, who pauses to fuss with the garbage can and am immediately enveloped in chilled air and murky shadows.

"Come here," my mother calls. "I have a surprise for you."

I open my mouth, close it again, and go dutifully into the living room doorway. The sliding glass curtain is closed and Barry White is on the CD player.

"Here's a hint," she purrs and I track her disembodied voice to the swivel rocker facing away from me. "Think back twenty-seven years, to the presents you gave me the night you asked me to be your girlfriend. I was so excited that I wore them almost every day for six months straight, remember? Well, guess what?" She spins the chair around to show off an ancient green-and-white softball cap and team jersey. "Recognize these?"

No I don't, but the colors are familiar, seeing as how

the entire Estertown school system, from kindergarten through high school, still uses them.

Her flirtatious gaze meets my anguished one and in the split second before she snaps upright a medley of shock, guilt, and anger contort her features. "Meredith! What are you doing here? I told you supper wasn't until six!"

"I found her outside," my father says, coming up and settling his hands on my shoulders. "I thought it would be nice if we finally got a chance to talk."

"Talk?" my mother says. "Now? But I thought we were going to—"

"Plans have changed." My father's fingers dig into my skin, preventing me from bolting. "We'll discuss this later, Sharon."

"Later? Later when? We're supposed to be together *now*. You know I'm ovulating—"

"Sharon!"

"Oh, she already knows we're trying to get pregnant," my mother snaps, glaring at me like I interrupted them on purpose. "Or at least we're *supposed* to be trying."

I've heard enough, but my father's hands pin me and the moaning in my head still isn't loud enough to drown out what comes next.

"What about yesterday?" he says.

"Once! One time. Big deal," my mother says sulkily.

"Once is all it takes," my father says.

134

"So that's it? That's my reward for waiting three years?" The chair creaks. "That's not fair, Charles. I'm doing everything I can for you. You *know* I am."

"Keep it down, will you?" my father says. "The neighbors."

"Oh, screw the neighbors," she cries. "I don't care about them, I care about us!"

"Well, if you care about *me,* you'll shut up before somebody calls the cops," he says, releasing me and striding over to her.

"Oh," she says, sounding stricken. "I'm sorry. I forgot."

Somehow my brain's frantic signals reach my legs. I turn and with robotic stiffness, walk straight to my bedroom. Enter. Close the door. Lock it.

Seconds later my father tries the knob. "Meredith? Open the door."

"No," I say.

"Open the door. I want to talk to you."

I shake my head. I don't care if he can't hear me. I walk around the bed and perch on the edge of the mattress, watching the doorknob jiggle.

Click.

The door opens.

My father comes into my room and stops in front of me. Holds up a thin, metal rod, the all-purpose key to open any all-purpose door. "I'm not going through a repeat of this

135

morning's little adventure. From now on, no more locked doors around here, okay?"

I round my shoulders and consider my feet. Reach over to the nightstand and pluck the bottle of black nail polish from the rainbow assortment. Tuck my knee beneath my chin, unscrew the cap, and begin painting. Dab, dab. Short strokes. My hair interferes with my concentration so I tuck it behind my ears. Hiding behind the curtain doesn't matter now because my face muscles are paralyzed and my eyes have seen their fill.

"Meredith," my father says softly. "Chirp."

Dab, dab.

He sits down next to me. His body radiates heat and the faint scent of my mother's CK Obsession cologne. He waits. Sighs.

Short strokes. I exceed the nail's limit and paint a glossy, black streak across the top of my toe. I leave it there. Do it again and again.

"Look, I know you're upset," he murmurs, touching my arm. "I don't blame you. Your mother wasn't supposed to tell you about this new baby. I wanted to tell you myself and I would have if you hadn't skipped out on me this morning."

I move on to the next toe and don't even try to stay within the lines.

"You know nobody could ever take your place," he says,

toying with the skeleton key. "Believe me, this new baby won't come between us. We'll take care of it together, I have it all figured out. We'll teach it shapes and colors and ABCs. . . ."

I remember his ABC game. I had to sit on his lap and whisper in his ear, repeating one foul word after another in alphabetical order.

Shaking, I stick the nail wand back into the bottle. Slip my hand into my right pocket and press the teddy cam remote. Scratch my thigh and, without looking at him, continue painting my toes. My duplicity feels huge and obvious. My face burns.

"Chirp? What're you doing? You're making a mess."

I blink and find three perfectly round blobs of black polish spotting the pink floral comforter. I move my heel and smear it into the dainty weave.

"Don't do that. Your mother'll have a fit. Do you have any nail polish remover?" His hand lights on my back. "No? We'll keep it our secret, then." He caresses the curve of my spine. "When did you start wearing a bra, baby?"

My head droops. I become a marble statue as his trembling fingers twitch to my side, dip under my armpit, and pause, spasming, at the curve of my breast.

His breath hitches. "Oh God," he whispers, then exhales in a stale rush and closes his fingers around me and—

"Charles?"

He snatches his hand away.

"Charles?" my mother calls again. "I thought you were going to be right back."

He clears his throat. Quietly. "I'm coming, Sharon."

The mattress springs up as he rises. The gauze knee patch flexes and fresh scrapes tic-tac-toe his shins. Desire rolls off him in waves, a deadly, invisible gas that will strike me down unless I take the necessary precautions.

I should have taken my vitamins today.

"I wish I didn't have to go." He lingers, stroking my hair. "Promise you'll be here when I get back?"

I nod once, slowly, but don't look up.

"Okay, then, let me go do this," he says and adds apologetically, "I have to shut your door. Your mother wants this private." He pauses in front of me, too close. "Hey, what if after dinner you and I go down to the Dairy Queen for some ice cream—"

"No," I say loudly.

"Charles?" my mother calls.

"Coming," he says hurriedly.

I listen to the *swish* and *snick* as the door closes. Wait, motionless, until their muffled voices rise and fall beneath the throbbing bass.

Then I shut off the camera and climb out the window.

chapter seventeen

I drop to the ground and stumble but don't fall.

Mrs. Calvinetti watches from her porch. She hisses and makes arthritic hand signs to ward off my evil. The twins have abandoned their soccer melee and now roll around the front lawn, locked in mortal combat. They grunt and curse and practice wrestling moves on each other. When they see me they stop fighting, hitch up their baggy shorts, and call, "Hey, how's your faggot father? Did he blow any kids today?"

Mrs. Calvinetti scolds them shrilly in Italian.

The Mobile Mechanic's gone and Nigel's Buick is parked near Andy's steps.

I head for the court out of habit. I can see and hear but I don't feel anything and I wonder vaguely if my mind has closed down to keep me from opening my pocketknife and ending this whole stupid mess with one swipe.

I stop walking and look at my wrists. They need washing.

I sink onto the curb, sick with the realization that I have nowhere left to run to, that I can't get away, and with the exception of my grandmother across town, my entire life spans a distance no greater than that of the condo complex and, more specifically, the Dumpster court.

I'm like a pinball bouncing off the same people over and over again, flinging myself around in a desperate attempt to avoid disappearing into the black hole of my father's embrace . . .

"My daddy," I whisper, staring up at the four big white ceiling tiles framed within the curtain track. "I don't want him to get in trouble. I just want him to stop."

"Shhh, it's all right." The lady with the velvet eyes warms my frigid hands. "You're safe now. We're not going to let anything happen to you." Her voice is soothing, but she's wearing rubber gloves and the smell turns my stomach.

I gulp and concentrate on the ceiling. One two three four, my gaze travels from corner to corner, over and over again. The tiles are white, the curtain is white. The sheets on this bed are white, too, just like the ones at home were before. . . . My breath hitches. "He's gonna be mad. I wasn't supposed to tell."

"Tell what, sweetie?" the lady says softly, exchanging glances with the quieter lady on the other side of the bed who is doing something prickly to my arm.

I shake my head and think of white. Clouds are white, cotton is white. I need two more to make four. I need to cry but I can't. Oh. Snow and eggs. Am I still bleeding? I don't think so. There were doctors here, but now they're out talking to my mother. The look in her eyes as they took her out said, "Quiet, be quiet." I tried, I will tell her. I tried, but I couldn't.

I'm up and moving again, running headlong into the smothering heat.

I won't bleed for him anymore.

Parking lot pebbles gouge my heels, sweat streams from my pores.

My mother's giving him another baby.

"What did you tell them?" my mother whispers, stepping back in and bending over me after the velvet-eyed lady leaves, and she and I are now alone behind the rippling white curtain. "You didn't mention Daddy, did you?"

The drugs stretch me see-through and I drift above myself, touching the four tiles, wondering why she needs me to talk when she can see the answer in my head.

"You didn't blame him, did you?" Her breath is sour in my nostrils. "You know he didn't mean it, he loves you, he really does. It was a mistake, Meredith, so nobody's really to blame. You understand that, don't you?"

"I told them," I mumble, floating like a wispy, white cloud.

"You told them?" She isn't whispering anymore. "How could you do that? Don't you know what's going to happen?" Her fingers

*yank me down from the peaceful place. "We're supposed to stick to-
gether, family is supposed to stick together. He made a mistake! Lots
of people make mistakes and no one tells on them! How could you?"*

*The curtain swishes open. "Mrs. Shale? Your daughter needs
rest."*

*"Don't touch me," my mother growls, clinging to my arm.
"Meredith, tell them you were wrong, tell them you lied. Go ahead,
tell them."*

"Here she is, guys," the nurse says grimly. "Be my guest."

*My mother yelps and walkie-talkies squawk and the bed pitches
and jerks, but everything is smudgy and distant and dark as I float
away. . . .*

I pound across the burning macadam, an eighteen-
wheeler running at full throttle, past Andy's and then right
back up the hot, metal steps to his door. The curtains
twitch and I find myself returning Nigel's gaze.

"You arrested my father that day," I say as he lets me in.
My eyes don't adjust to the darkness quickly enough and
the air-conditioning makes my head spin. I stumble and
Nigel steers me into a seat. "Tell me again what you saw
and this time I want details. No more of that 'we got the
call, arrested him, and that was it' crap. I was in the middle
of it, remember? If that didn't kill me, this won't, either." I
smear sweat from my forehead and drain the glass of water
Ms. Mues offers.

"Now?" Clearly uncomfortable, Nigel runs a ham-size

hand over his hair and trudges back to the table. He sits and the cushioned chair wheezes beneath him.

"What's going on with you, Mer?" Andy asks and his hands close tight around the Jim Beam bottle. He looks like he wishes he were already in Iowa.

And that pisses me off because I *can't* run away to Iowa or to Leah Louisa's or drown myself in alcohol. I have to stay to protect others and keep my wits sharp to protect myself. "My father and mother are trying to have another baby."

Andy hoists his bottle and drinks.

chapter eighteen

There's more." I go to the sink and wash my hands. Push the words out over the sound of the water. "He touched my . . . above the waist. Over my shirt. The camera was on." I cringe at the thought of everyone seeing my humiliation.

"Camera?" Ms. Mues asks.

Nigel explains the nanny cams while I rinse the soap away.

"When I got home before, my mother was in the living room. He told me to wait in my room while they messed around." I scrape myself with paper towels. My hands and wrists are clean, but the rest of me still feels filthy.

Nigel's brows hang low over his eyes. "You're telling me he groped you and now that kinky son of a bowlegged hamster and your mother are going at it in the living room?" He shoves his chair from the table and his footsteps rattle the dishes in the cabinets. "Will somebody tell me what the *hell* it's gonna take to get this guy a one-way ticket out of here?"

"Nothing, because nobody cares," Andy says, staring at the ceiling. "No matter what he does or how many kids he ruins, he's still a human being and he still has rights under the law. He's *sick,* and because he is, we're screwed." His fingers are busy twisting the bottle cap off and on, off and on. "God sure does work in mysterious ways, huh, Ma?"

"Please," Ms. Mues says, distressed. "The unjust shall be punished, if not in this world, then in the next."

Andy snorts. "Don't hold your breath."

"My grandmother was hoping he'd be murdered in prison," I say to get him to look at me. It doesn't work and I feel like kicking him. I probably would if his mother and Nigel weren't there.

Ms. Mues stares worriedly at Andy. "Please don't start questioning your faith. Not now, when you're so close to a cure." She glances at Nigel. "There must be something we can do. Touching Meredith *must* have violated the terms of Charles's probation—"

"No offense, Paula, but how about joining us in the real world for a minute?" He shakes his head, looks us over, and heaves a resigned sigh. "Oh, all right. Little girl goes to the ER. The mother doesn't want her kid talking to the doctors. The cops are called in. The kid talks to the rape counselor while they're swabbing up DNA samples."

Andy sets the bottle on the table and leans forward in his chair, plants his elbows on his knees, and stares at the floor. His T-shirt is dark with sweat.

I wish he would look at me.

"The detectives question the mother, who's looking to lawyer right up, while me and my partner head over to the house to grab this . . ." His face twists. "To grab up old Chuckie. He doesn't answer the door, so we kick it in and find him stuffing bloody sheets into the washing machine. 'Course that's not gonna do nothing about the blood smeared all over his shorts and legs, though, is it?"

Ms. Mues makes a low, wounded-animal sound and glances at Andy, who is staring stonily at his feet.

I didn't know about the washing machine. I wasn't in court for the entire case and know nothing of the others' testimony. All I know is that shame and shock sealed my throat when the most sordid details of the story needed telling.

"When I read him his rights and ask what he's doing, he says he's trying to save his daughter the embarrassment of seeing how heavy her first period was." Sarcasm shreds his words. "Seems it caught her by surprise."

"He said *that*?" I blurt, stung and weirdly embarrassed. "What a liar."

"Yeah, well, it goes with the territory. Anyhow, he isn't exactly cooperative, so now we have to use a little reasonable force," Nigel says with a grim smile. "I'm kneeling on his back and my partner's cuffing him and he's cursing away, but by the time we hit the squad car he's bawling, telling us how sick he is and how much he hates himself."

"I can't deal with this," Andy says abruptly. He jams the bottle between his legs, wheels, and whips out of the room.

Slowly, cheeks burning, I untuck my hair and dip my head.

"I'm sorry, Meredith," Ms. Mues says, touching my clenched hands.

"Feel sorry for *him*." I say loudly. "The details are real and if he won't face them, then what's the difference between him and my mother? She won't deal with what really happened, either."

"Fuck you, Meredith!" Andy shouts from his room.

I'm up and out of my chair before his voice fades, down the hall and into his bedroom, lashing out and kicking him, bruising numb flesh that doesn't even flinch. The sound of the vicious blows fuels my frenzy because I want him to feel it, all of it, and he won't. He can't.

But I don't want to be the only one.

"Don't ever say that again," he says, fumbling with his wheels. "You think you know, Meredith, but you don't." He spins away from me, his knuckles skeleton white on the metal rims. "Christ, I wish I was in Iowa!"

I reach out, grab his braid, and jerk him to a brutal halt. See my own clenched fist yanking taut the woven rope. Drop it and step back.

"I can't stay here, Mer. Don't you get that yet?" he says hoarsely, reaching around and rubbing his scalp. "I'm useless. I know what he did to you and to me and to all those other kids and I still don't have the balls to do anything about it!" His voice cracks. "I see him walking around out there all free and cocky and I swear to Christ, I want to rip his heart out. But I can't." His chin sinks to his chest. "I can't even look at him."

Our backs are to the mirror and we're temporarily blessed with no reflections. I can see the oak Madonna, though, and smell the scent of roses mingled with the fear seeping from Andy's skin. I put my fingertips against his temples and feel his pulse jittering beneath them.

"I *begged* him not to do it and it didn't matter," he whispers. "I trusted him and he screwed me. Told me I could call him Dad in private . . . he called me Buddy and I thought it was so cool that he'd given me a nickname, you know? I thought it meant he really liked me." A shudder rips through him. "And then he got me. He took my power and when he went to prison I thought I had it back, but I don't. I don't." He breaks and weeps like a little boy.

I look to the Blessed Virgin, but she keeps her counsel. I

stroke Andy's back and bowed neck. There's nothing I can say to comfort him because he's right. My father trapped us in time and we will always be small around him.

"Meredith?" Ms. Mues fills the doorway. Her face sags like bread dough. She motions me out of the room and toward the kitchen.

I rest my cheek against Andy for a moment, then step away.

He doesn't ask me to stay. Maybe doesn't even know I'm gone.

I follow her back to the kitchen and take my seat. I can still hear him crying.

Ms. Mues and Nigel sit across from me like mourners at a wake.

"When Andy started getting hurt, I thought he was just at the awkward age little boys go through. All arms and legs and no coordination," Ms. Mues says, staring down at her fingers. "I figured he'd outgrow it. You know how kids are. One day, he was climbing a tree behind the old house and I was doing the dishes and watching him out the window. He kept going higher and higher. I got nervous because he *was* accident-prone and if he fell from that height. . . . Well, I was just about to call him when he inched out onto a limb and just . . . let go."

I light a cigarette.

"I begged God to spare him and miraculously he survived the fall with only two broken ribs and a broken collarbone. I didn't tell the doctors what I'd seen. Maybe I should have, but all I wanted to do was protect him. His father was dead, the man I had brought into our home was pulling away from us, and I thought Andy was heartbroken at losing him. I didn't know what was going on, I swear."

The curling smoke makes my eyes water.

"When Andy got out of the hospital he begged me not to leave him alone," she says, voice faint. "He said he couldn't breathe while I was gone. When I finally had to go back to work he went hysterical and told me about your father."

Nigel curses under his breath.

"I could have killed Charles with my bare hands. I'd trusted him, given him carte blanche to my son. He'd lied to me about everything." Her voice fades and she resurrects it. "I wanted to have him arrested, but Andy begged me not to. He didn't want anybody to know. He said if the kids at school found out they'd call him a 'gay boy' and a 'faggot' and nobody would hang around with him anymore."

"Kids are great, huh?" Nigel mutters.

"What about counseling? I thought you took him to a psychologist or something," I say, crushing out my cigarette in the brimming ashtray.

151

"I did." Ms. Mues sounds exhausted. "We went after I told Charles that if I ever heard even a whisper of his touching another child I would see him in hell."

"Fat lot of good that did." The malice in my voice shocks me. Am I mad at her, too? Do I blame *everyone* for not protecting me?

"We had a saying in the army," she whispers, staring down at her hands. " 'God hates a coward.' " Her chin trembles. "I pray every night for the opportunity to redeem myself." She meets my gaze. "And now this."

"Which kind of brings me back to my original point," Nigel says. "Four years ago we had a traumatized little girl and a confession from her father. We had a couple of other kids swearing on a stack of Bibles that he'd wronged them, too. We had bloody sheets and DNA evidence. Medical records on Meredith's injuries. We had everything to make this an open-and-shut case."

I pick up the saltshaker. Chip a spot of dried tomato sauce from Mary's painted robe. Set her down.

"The lawyers start blowing smoke. We get character witnesses for old Chuck stretching all the way back to when he was a high school baseball star. We get 'expert testimony' from a two-thousand-dollar-a-day rent-a-shrink hired by the defense. We get two little boys who go hysterical when they're asked to point to who did this to them."

"I didn't know that," I interrupt. Two boys crumble on the stand while I, the daughter, the one with everything to lose, finger him without a hiccup.

"Yeah, it was a circus." Nigel's face creases with disgust. "The town wanted it over fast on account of your granny being mayor and all, but your mother didn't. She gave the paper some big sob story about false accusations and how sad it was that the mayor's daughter had to sell her house to pay for the defense."

So that was why we moved into the condo. Not to spare me bad memories, but to save my father from prison.

Nigel stabs out his cigarette and squints fiercely through the lingering smoke. "The point being, Paula, is that praying is all well and good, but it doesn't do squat for us right now. We need hard evidence because if we had him dead to rights last time—and we did—and he was sentenced to nine years and he *still* got out in three, then what the hell do you think he's gonna get for groping one teenager on video, even if she *is* his daughter?"

I stare down at my hands. Hear Andy's chair moving over the bare wood floors of his room and the faint strains of "Little Green Apples." I don't know what to say or do now that Nigel has banished our illusions and Andy has bailed out.

"So that's it?" Ms. Mues says.

"I'm afraid so," Nigel says. "There's nothing we can do except wait until that lying sack of llama turds gets serious—"

"*No!*" Ms. Mues is on her feet and the chair goes over backward, landing with a crash. "What does he have to do, attack Meredith *again*?"

"Do you really think I want to see that happen?" Nigel says, glaring at her from beneath his brows. "Christ, Paula, the point is to nail this guy once and for all." He rises and lumbers, swearing, about the room.

"I wish he would just die," I hear myself say and draw back as they stop and stare at me. "What?" I burn under the heat of their combined gazes. "Oh, come on. Like nobody's really wishing that but me."

Ms. Mues and Nigel exchange looks. Something dark passes between them.

"Meredith, he's your father," she says. "You don't really wish he was dead."

A sharp, sudden thrill of fear makes the hair on my arms rise. We are three and three is the number of initial completion, the first stage achieved. We need only harness our dark, unspoken desires to become four—

"Yeah, well, get the idea of your old man croaking right out of your head because it ain't gonna happen,"

Nigel says, hitching up his baggy pants. "I saw him running around out there, remember? He's as healthy as a damn ox."

I blink. Shrug. Okay, I can play along. Pretend I'm the only one hoping for a permanent solution. "So maybe he'll get hit by a car, or swallow wrong and choke." I *knew* I shouldn't have thrown away those steaks. Whenever somebody chokes, it's *always* on a hunk of steak.

Ms. Mues and Nigel are talking, but I'm caught up in the fantasy of my father's permanent absence. It's a siren song that promises peace and remains maddeningly out of reach.

"His kind live forever," Nigel mutters.

His words snatch the dream right out from under me.

Ms. Mues pats me. "Don't fret, honey. God works in mysterious ways."

I don't even have the strength left to deny her words. To open my mouth and agree with Nigel, because as hope dissolves it gives me a glimpse of what my life is going to be like with my father and without Andy. I run my thumb along the outline of the knife in my pocket and wonder why I just don't use it.

Maybe because my mother would have heart failure at the sight of blood splattering her shiny white whirlpool tub and I don't want irritation to be her last memory of me. Or maybe I'm afraid my father will be the one to find me, and if I'm dead or dying, I won't be able to fight off his last invasion.

I don't know. I've learned too much today and can't hold myself steady. I have no balance left. I should have taken my vitamins.

"Meredith?" Andy calls. "Can you come here a minute?"

"Yes," I say and go to him because it might be the last time.

The silence in the kitchen follows me down the hall.

Andy's face is swollen and blotchy. He has a key ring in one hand, his bottle in the other. The giant oak Madonna lies across his lap. Stray wisps of hair escape his braid and cling to his cheeks.

I perch on the bed. Memorize his face so when I close my eyes I can still find him. My wonderful, three-year vacation is over. The pressure in my chest cracks my ribs and floods my bloodstream, swelling my arteries to capacity.

"We'll be out of here early tomorrow morning." He places the ring in my palm and closes my fingers over it. "I'm leaving you my keys, just in case."

"In case of what?" I ask numbly.

"I don't know, anything," he says, shrugging and avoiding my gaze. "In case you need a place to hole up."

"You're not coming back." My head pounds as I pocket

the keys. "That's why you're taking her with you." My fingertips burn against the Blessed Virgin's smooth, wooden face. If she had working eyelids, I would close them. This is no time for witnesses.

"I'm coming back," he says, but his color deepens as he hurriedly hefts her onto my lap. "I was just gonna leave her with you in case you . . . I don't know." His fingers intertwine with mine. "Need her, I guess."

I want to ask if he still loves me, but I'm not sure I can deal with either answer. The patchouli incense has gone out and the rose scent is fading. The CD has stopped. The weight of the Virgin Mother rests heavy across my thighs, and I don't know what to do about any of it. These are four dark omens.

"Thank you." The girl in the mirror stares back at me with no expression. "I didn't take my vitamins today." So many loose ends to share before it's over. Who will I talk to after this? "Did I tell you that the first present my father ever gave my mother was a baseball shirt?" I glance at his pained expression. "No, I guess I didn't. Well, it was. Funny, huh?" I dig my lighter from my pocket and hold the trembling flame to the tip of the incense stick. "He's the one who wants the new baby, you know. She doesn't. She'll just do anything to keep him. Probably even look the other way the next time he comes after me." I get down on my hands and knees and sniff the edges of the room, searching for the failing air freshener that isn't giving me my roses. "I *know* she won't take me to the hospital again because then he'll be arrested."

"Meredith, please get up," he says, wheeling closer to me.

"I can't." I crawl along the base moldings. "You should play the Dino CD some more, Andy. I think that song is starting to grow on me." I spy an outlet and for one brief flash see myself sticking the tip of the knife into one of the slots. But I don't, because frying will make me smell awful. "Do you know that I've never had a pet? Not even a goldfish. Isn't that sad?" I sit up on my haunches and sniff the air. Patchouli but no roses. "Are you really coming back on Wednesday?"

"Yes," he says after a heartbeat.

"But it's not gonna be the same." I brush a dust bunny from my overalls.

"I can't live near him, Meredith," he says quietly. "I know my mother has this grand plan about haunting him for the rest of her life, but that's *her* atonement, not mine. If he disappeared off the face of the earth tomorrow I'd stay here forever, but he won't, so *I* have to. Move, I mean."

I find another dust bunny and add it to the first. Roll them together into a ball.

"You want to come with me?" he asks, gliding over to me.

No. I want him to stay here. "If I leave he'll target some other kid and I can't deal with that. Knowing that I just let it happen." He doesn't ask how I'm going to stop it from happening, though, and my heart curls in on itself. My father has stolen Andy's soul and broken all his defenses except flight. "And besides, my grandmother would pull every string she could to find me and then you'd get in trouble for harboring a runaway and end up going to jail for twenty years."

"Yeah, I thought of that." He strokes my hair and I wilt against his chair, listening to the familiar gurgle as he upends the bottle of Jim Beam. "I'd risk it if you were closer to eighteen, but three years is a long time to lay low."

"Mm-hmm." I tug up his pant leg and inspect the pale flesh. Puffy, plum-purple bruises are already forming beneath the fine, brown leg hair. I touch each stormy splotch and wonder if the victim soul in Iowa will heal these for him, too, or if they'll stay as souvenirs, aging to a sickly greenish yellow by Wednesday.

"Good thing I can't feel them, huh?" he jokes, but his voice hitches and dies.

I wonder if he's scared of losing this shield that protects him from physical pain and what Ms. Mues will do with her life when my father is back in prison for good. I wonder if Nigel will be able to claim the role of arresting officer again, even though he's retired, and if my mother will ever grow sick of the taste of shame and seek a divorce.

And I wonder if she will ever forgive me for what I'm about to set into motion.

"I have to go now," I say and release Andy as my anchor.

The Blessed Mother watches as we kiss good-bye, as he crushes the air from my lungs, releases me, and wheels away, hobbled by his own fear-born failure.

We exchange glances, the icon and I, but we don't weep.

There is no place here for miracles.

chapter nineteen

Nigel and Ms. Mues go quiet as I enter the kitchen.

I hug her good-bye and wish her luck in Iowa. I hope for both their sakes that the trip spurs Andy's recovery. I don't say it, but I really don't expect to see her again. She'll come home on Wednesday, but by then it'll all be over and I have no idea where or *if* I will even be.

Nigel watches hard as I shake the curtain closed over my face. He sees something before I disappear, though, and says roughly, "Don't push for an end here, kid. Trust me, I've been around this block before and it'll all play out. You just hang in there a little longer, okay? Don't go doing anything stupid."

"I won't," I say and step out the door into the oven.

The sun is slinking off to the west but the heat remains, shimmying up from the baked macadam and drawing the moisture from my skin. The Dumpster court reeks.

I force myself up the side lawn and around the front. Stop with my hand on the doorknob and wonder if I should knock before entering or somehow slip unnoticed back into my room. I don't know how to engineer my own destruction.

The knob twists beneath my fingers and the door flies open. My mother jerks to a halt. "Oh! There you are." She gives the Madonna icon a quick frown, grabs my arm, and says, "Go inside right now and change. We're going out to dinner."

I wait for mention of our last confrontation, but she's already calling my father's condo to report my return.

"I don't want to go," I say as she hangs up the phone. "Why don't you two just go have dinner without me?"

"Because this is our first time out together as a family and your father wants you with us," my mother says, brushing a speck of lint from her pink linen dress. "Now go get ready. I bought you an outfit. Put it on."

"I don't want to," I say, setting down the Blessed Virgin and beginning my vitamin ritual. I swallow my lifesaving pills in lots of four, but the number denies me its usual comfort, leaving me sloshing with V8 and slightly nauseous.

Her fingernails tap the countertop. "Do you have to argue with everything I say? Can't you just say 'okay, Mom' one time? Is that too much to ask?"

"If I have to go I want to wear my own stuff," I say, stifling a burp.

She takes my empty glass and sets it in the sink. "Meredith, so help me, I've just about had it with you today. Now, go into your room and put on the outfit I bought you or we're going to have a serious problem. And take that thing with you," she adds irritably, gesturing to the Madonna. "It's getting on my nerves." She waits but I don't move. "Well? What're you waiting for?"

"Your face makeup's cracking," I say, motioning to the frown lines in her forehead. "I think it's on too thick."

I watch as my mother slides the shimmering, pink lipstick across her lips. She swishes on blush and bends down, touching the soft brush to my cheeks. "Ooh, you're so beautiful now, Meredith. Just like a grown-up lady."

"Like Cinderella?" I say, staring up into her beloved face.

"Better than Cinderella," she says, laughing because she knows what's coming next.

"Like you?" I say, beaming.

"Oh, better than me," she says, lightly pinching my cheek.

"Nobody's better than you, Mommy," I say, seizing and smooching the back of her slim, perfumed hand. . . .

Hurt creases her face and she runs for the bedroom.

Slowly, I cap the last vitamin bottle and put it back into the cabinet. Any satisfaction I feel in besting my mother is tempered by the ghostly sweep of a blusher brush against my hot cheek. The memory shakes something loose inside of me and it rattles in my hollow chest.

"You'd better get moving," she calls from the bedroom.

"Okay, Mom." I put the icon on my nightstand and head for the shower. Emerge minutes later and slip into my bedroom. Lock the door.

The outfit my mother laid out for me is big, awful, and beige. A boxy cotton jacket, a baggy white blouse, and of all things, tailored, knee-length walking shorts. Good thing I shaved my legs at Leah Louisa's.

I don the clothes. Study myself in the mirror.

With the exception of my tangled bed head, I blend right into the walls.

I slip my knife in my pocket, my cigarettes, and the remotes in my purse.

When I enter the kitchen, my mother hides a swift, satisfied smile. "You look very nice," she says, smoothing her own dress. "Let's go."

"Thanks." I know she's lying, but I don't mind looking ugly if it will repel my father for a few more hours.

I follow her out to the car, climb into the backseat, and swelter until the air-conditioning reaches me. The leather makes my butt sweat and if this keeps up my shorts will be dripping by the time we get to the restaurant. Lucky me, I'll be more repugnant than even my mother could have hoped for.

We cruise through the complex to my father's. Nigel's

car is back in his own parking lot and I can see Gilly watching the world go by from the picture window.

My mother pulls into a spot and toots the horn.

My father, handsome and respectable in Gap khakis and a button-down plaid, comes out onto the porch.

"Aren't you even a little glad he's back, Mer?" my mother says softly, watching him follow the sidewalk toward us.

I look at him and the only answer is *if.* If he hadn't. If he didn't. If.

Andy says he stole our power, but that's just part of it.

He taught me how to wish him gone forever.

He opens the front passenger door and a gust of hot, gritty air sweeps in.

"This must be my lucky day," he says, sliding into the seat. "Dining out with my beautiful wife and daughter; who could ask for more than that?"

"You're so silly," my mother simpers, leaning over for a kiss. "But I love you."

He ignores me—punishment, I guess, for running away a second time—and spends the ride charming my mother instead.

And Andy's right; each word my father speaks is a shove, a mocking reminder that I am small and weak enough to be used without regard, and that I was.

165

My mother turns up the CD player. "When a Man Loves a Woman" grates out.

My father flips down his vanity mirror under the pretense of checking his clean-shaven chin for stubble, but he is actually looking at me.

I know this because I can feel the force of his gaze probing my curtain for cracks. I don't move, so he finally gives up and closes the mirror.

"That is *such* a good song," my mother says, sighing as it ends.

I don't ask if she's completely delusional when she pulls into Steakhouse Sam's crowded parking lot. I don't remind her that Sam had a son in the Boys' League who missed my father's coaching by a month, or that Sam is an ex-marine with a low boiling point.

"Steakhouse Sam's," my father muses. "I've missed this place."

"I haven't been here since you left," my mother says. "We used to have such good times here so I figured what better place to begin again?"

They *are* delusional, I decide as I follow them across the parking lot, up the steps, and into the foyer. They don't notice the whiplash double takes we're receiving or hear the bass rumble beneath the restaurant's cheerful clatter.

"Sam!" my mother cries, swinging up to the front desk. "How are you?"

The stocky guy goes still. His gaze flickers past my sparkling mother and settles, hardening, on my father. Slowly, he reaches up and removes the pen tucked behind his ear. "Sorry. We're full up tonight."

"Oh, we don't mind waiting," my mother burbles, glancing over her shoulder at my father. "We've been dreaming of your steaks for—"

"I'm sorry," Sam says expressionlessly. "You'll have to go somewhere else."

My mother's smile turns bewildered. "What?" She cocks her head as if to hear him better. "I mean, do you take reservations now or—"

"We're full up tonight," Sam says.

My mother turns to my father. "Charles?"

He steps forward and the air around us buzzes like hornets. "C'mon, Sam," he says but his heartiness is forced. "You sure you couldn't squeeze us in?"

"I'm asking you to vacate the premises," Sam says, holding my father's glittering gaze. He raps the pen against the desk. Once. Twice. Three times. "If you don't leave right now, I'll get the cops to escort you out of here."

I edge closer to the door.

"Fine." My father grabs my mother's arm. Wheels and stalks out.

I scurry after them into the humid night.

My father mutters a stream of curses through the parking lot and as we're pulling out, he gives the crowd lingering on the steps both middle fingers.

"Charles," my mother warns, glancing in her rearview mirror.

"Don't lecture me, Sharon," he says, staring out his window. "What the hell is wrong with this town, anyway? Christ, they used to *love* me. I was the only one who could get their kids to play decent ball. I led them to *three* winning seasons and now, what? I'm some kind of freak?" A muscle ties in his jaw. "I never should have come back here."

"Don't say that," my mother says.

"I mean it," he says. "I'm not staying here any longer than I have to."

The air in the car is suddenly heavy and still.

"What are you saying?" my mother asks.

He shoots her an irritated look. "What am I, not speaking English? I'm saying I'm not spending the rest of my life in this dump, that's what. We're going to have to move."

"Move?" my mother says, exhaling in a rush. He has used the "we" word and now she knows she's not being abandoned. "Hmm, that might not be a bad idea. Then we really *could* make a new start."

I sink low in the backseat, wrinkling my frumpy outfit, but it doesn't matter. I'm being buried alive in my parents' mass grave and now all bets are off.

We dine at the new Olive Garden up on the highway where no one knows us.

I eat salad and get dressing in my hair.

My father hisses in revulsion when I wipe it from the strands, but as we're walking to the car afterward and my mother is searching her purse for her keys, he lags behind and presses briefly against me.

"I love watching you walk," he whispers and his breath crisps the hair at the back of my neck.

My adrenaline spikes and my fingers close around the knife in my pocket.

He winks and ambles past to catch up with my mother. She smiles and slips her arm through his. Her tread is light and bouncy and I can almost see the ghost of her cheerleader's ponytail bobbing at the back of her head.

Slowly, I uncurl my fingers from around the knife. I keep my hands buried in my pockets, though, because the shaking will give me away.

He didn't choke on his lasagna and there isn't a drunk driver in sight.

There are only the three of us and our dark, burgeoning desires.

I am so afraid of what comes next.

chapter twenty

I see the flashing red lights while we're waiting to turn off Main Street.

"Looks like something happened in your building," my mother says and gazes at my father, missing two gaps in the stream of oncoming traffic that would have allowed her to turn into the complex.

My father shifts and yanks irritably at the seat belt's restraint.

"Charles?" my mother says as if waiting for instruction, as if all he has to do is say the word and she'll flick off her signal light and sail right past the complex and we will never, ever come home again.

"What?" he asks.

She clears her throat. "Did you really register today?"

My father stabs her with a scornful look. "Turn in already," he says, giving the finger to whoever is blowing the horn behind us. "Jesus Christ, Sharon, I *told* you I did, didn't I? What, are you gonna start now, too?"

"No, of course not. I'm sorry." She whips the car through a small break in traffic and zips into the complex. Brakes as a cop holds up his hand. "Charles, I think they're at your unit."

"They're *in* my unit," my father says and opens the car door.

"Wait till I pull over," my mother says and scrapes the tires along the curb. She struggles to free herself and catch up with him.

I scan the crowd and spot Nigel talking to a patrolman. He waves me over.

"What's going on?" I say as Gilly licks the sweat salt from my knees.

"Somebody redecorated the front of your old man's place with eggs and threw a cinderblock through the sliding glass door," Nigel said, tugging his pants up beneath his ponderous belly. "Took a dump on the back steps, too."

"Gross," I say.

"Stupid question, but can you think of anyone specific who might hold a grudge against your father?" the cop asks, keeping an ear cocked to his radio.

"Besides the whole town?" I shake my head. "I don't know."

"You were out tonight?" Nigel asks, giving my outfit a curious once-over.

"Yeah." I tell him about the scene in Steakhouse Sam's

172

and about my father giving everyone the finger as we left. "So I guess it could have been anyone because everybody hates us." I study Gilly's massive head. "He says he's not going to stay here. He wants us all to move away. Soon."

Nigel narrows his eyes and lights a cigarette.

"Meredith!" My father jogs up, grabs my arm, and glowers at Nigel. "Leave her alone. She doesn't know anything. Why aren't you out there trying to catch who did this instead of interrogating children?"

"We're following up on several leads right now," the patrolman says coldly.

"Yeah, well, I want to know who's going to clean up this mess," my father says.

"So do we, Chuckles," Nigel says, exhaling a stream of smoke. "'Cause it's a hell of a welcome home from your fan club, isn't it?"

I can feel the hatred radiating from my father and try to tug free of his grasp, but he only tightens his grip. "Ow."

Nigel's gaze dips. "You want to let her go before we start seeing bruises where there weren't any five minutes ago?"

My father's churning anger drags me down and holds me beneath the surface until I'm inches from panic. It's all I can do not to lose myself in the standoff.

And then his hand falls away and he laughs self-consciously. "Sorry, guys. I guess I'm just really freaked over this." He waves in the direction of the condo. "Are there any witnesses?"

"Not so far," the patrolman says, pulling a pad from his shirt pocket and making a note on the page. "Nigel heard the crash and called it in, but the super says most of the units in your building are vacant. Nobody's home at the two occupied." The cop glances at him. "Anyone want you gone?"

"Besides everyone?" my father jokes, but his jaw is tight and he looks across the grass to where my mother is talking to another cop. Her arms are folded and her chin high. "I don't know. This isn't the town I used to know, that's for sure."

"Town's the same decent place it always was," Nigel says flatly.

I watch Gilly root through her stomach fluff for an errant flea.

"Why don't I take you home, Meredith?" my father says. "There's no point in your hanging around here."

"I'll walk her home," Nigel says.

"No," my father says.

"We're going to need you here to finish our report, Mr. Shale," the cop says. "We need to know if anything in the condo is missing—"

"Then her mother can take her home," my father says.

"Gilly needs walking anyway," Nigel says, crushing his cigarette out. "C'mon, kid." He tugs the dog's leash and she scrambles to her feet. "It's no bother at all."

My father is outgunned and hates it. "You can always stay here, Meredith."

"No, I'll go." I force myself to wait for Nigel plodding along beside me, but once we turn the curve, I light up. "So were you the one who trashed his place?"

"Me? Nah, that's kid stuff." He snorts out a laugh. "Can you really see me taking a dump right out there on—"

"Stop," I say, holding up a hand.

The light moment passes.

"Everything okay tonight?" Nigel asks as Gilly squats and pees.

"No." Andy's condo is dark and I see no silhouette in the living room window. Tomorrow he'll be gone. "He rubbed against me in the parking lot and said he loves to watch me walk."

"Cameras on?" Nigel asks, pausing at Andy's curb.

"They will be when I get there." I drop my cigarette and tap my pocketbook.

"You got Andy's keys, too, right? In case you need a place to hole up?"

I nod.

"Meredith?" Nigel waits until I meet his gaze. "Don't go

being a martyr. Anything happens, you either call me or 911." He runs a hand over his head and sighs. "I'll see if I can get a squad car to keep an eye on your place tonight."

"What, you think there's gonna be a lynch mob or something?" I look past the Cadillac and into the woods behind the fence. "Coming after my father?"

"It's not him I'm worried about. Flex a few beer muscles and that mob mentality takes over. They might decide to bomb you guys with something a little more lethal than eggs or bricks." His eyebrows knit together in a fearsome scowl. "Just watch your back, is all I'm saying."

"I will," I say and run up the steps. Go inside and lock the door. Sag against the wall until the jittering subsides. Wobble to my room. Lock the door. Change into drawstring cargo pants and an oversize T without putting on the light, just in case anyone is looking for targets. Fill the pockets with my life essentials, then drag my bulky beanbag chair in front of the door in case anyone tries to get at me in the night.

It's not enough. I need some kind of alarm that will trip at an attempted invasion. I have nothing but CDs and bottles of nail polish, so I stack them in a precarious pyramid on top of the beanbag chair, where a nudge will send them clattering to the carpet.

I make another pyramid beneath the locked window just

in case the mob sneaks a frontal attack through my sliced-up screen.

The air-conditioning is on but I'm sweating bad. The sharp scent of fear is known to arouse the predator's instincts so I rub patchouli oil onto my skin and hope it masks my weakness. I make a buffer wall of pillows and blankets on the window side of the bed to protect me from flying glass and cinderblock, then lie down and count my defenses.

Beanbag. Pyramids. Pillows.

The knife makes four.

I close my eyes to ease the burn and fall asleep with my hand in my pocket.

chapter twenty-one

I flutter on the edge of waking when the knock comes.

"Meredith?" my mother calls.

I open my eyes to streaming daylight.

"I know you're awake because you just stopped snoring," she says cheerfully. "Listen, your father and I are going down the shore; do you want to come with us?"

I sit up and rub my eyes. Clear my throat. "Uh, no. You guys go ahead."

"Are you sure?" my mother asks, sounding even more pleased.

"Yeah." I glance at the Madonna. Disassemble the pyramid so I can get out to pee. Call through the door, "What happened last night after I left?"

"Oh, the cops took all the information and then we had to wait for the maintenance guy to come and board up the sliding glass door. What a mess." But she doesn't sound like it was awful. In fact, she sounds way too happy.

"But he's still staying there, right?" I drag the chair away from the door.

"In that disaster? Of course not. The glass people are coming to fix the door tomorrow and your father's staying here in the meantime. And that's just between us, Meredith." A heartbeat of silence. "So, are you sure you don't want to come along?"

"Positive." I wait until she goes back to the kitchen to tell my father, then slip out, close the door behind me, and hustle into the bathroom.

They leave soon after that and I watch from the corner of my window until the car disappears around the blind curve. I wait, counting off four sets of twenty, but it doesn't return and the knot in my stomach loosens.

I make coffee and retrieve the Sunday paper from the stoop. The Calvinettis are loading beach chairs into their minivan and both grandsons give me the finger when their parents aren't watching.

How bizarre to think that when I stake myself out, it will be to save brats like them.

The thought stings and I push it away. Tomorrow belongs to betrayal. Today is mine and I don't want to waste it being afraid.

I make my camp out on the back patio. CD player, coffee, cranberry muffins. I put on my red bikini top and pull back my hair. My mother left her cellphone so I take that, too. Relax on a lounge and listen to the birds sing.

The only thing missing is Andy. How cool would it be to sit out here with him, drinking coffee and reading the funnies? We could talk and brush each other's hair while the sun colored us bronze and the air brushed away our scars.

I close my eyes and coax Andy from memory. Place him in the empty lounge next to mine. His walnut-shell brown eyes are soft and heavy-lidded, his hair spills down over his shoulders, and his legs are stretched out on the chair. I hold my breath as a buzzing fly lands on his bare toe, waiting to see if he'll twitch the pest away. The dark earth scent of patchouli rides the sudden breeze. . . .

"Close your eyes," Andy says, wheeling away from his bureau and over to where I'm sitting. "I have a surprise for you."

"Really?" I say, startled. "What is it?"

"You'll see," he says. "Now close your eyes and put out your hand."

I do and something cool, smooth, and rounded settles into my palm. "Can I look yet?"

"No," he says softly, from close, and kisses me. "Okay, look now."

It's a brand-new bottle of patchouli oil, the first gift any guy has ever bought me, the first he's bought me, and I don't know what to say.

181

"You said you liked it the first time you came over and we've been together a month now so I just thought . . ." He shrugs and flicks back his hair, trying for nonchalance, but when my smile breaks free his does, too. . . .

I sit up. Look across the court at his back door. The Cadillac is gone, the kitchen curtains are closed and still. Nothing stirs but the birds.

Iowa is so far away.

The muffins in my stomach ball into lead and my pants are sticky with sweat. Nigel's knife is in my pocket. I trace its outline and goose bumps rise on my skin.

I hate my father so much.

There is bold, bald truth in the ensuing silence; no one contradicts me or makes lame excuses for his behavior, no one urges me to forgive and forget, no one scolds or drops a noose fashioned of blood ties around my neck.

So I say it out loud. "I hate you so much."

"Say please," he murmurs, pressing against my trembling leg.

"Please," I whisper, eyes closed.

"Please what?"

I am supposed to say "please stop," but I know that when I do he'll just make animal noises and keep going, and I'll just lie here like a board and wait for it to be over.

"Please die," I say, closing my eyes and letting the sun bake the rancid, rotten Dumpster stench deep into my bones.

It is no worse than what I am about to receive.

chapter twenty-two

I try to keep busy, but I'm waiting for the end to begin and nothing really distracts me, not even calling and apologizing to Leah Louisa, who has left a slew of messages on the house machine and a few much more strident ones on my mother's voicemail. She's mad I skipped out on her yesterday, but after a minute of scolding I realize she's just scared that my father is going to get me before she can legally stop him.

I don't dare tell her that's the plan.

She complains that her lawyer cautioned her against moving me in without getting parental permission first, as the odds of successfully taking me away from them without documented cause are slim. She cheers up when she hears about Steakhouse Sam's, though, and the trashing of my father's condo.

I tell her how my father gave people the finger and said he wasn't staying in this miserable town and she says, "Good riddance," and goes off on a rant before I can say that if he goes, we all have to go with him. Then she asks where they are and I say the shore and she mutters, "Pray for a riptide," and I laugh because she expects me to, but when I hang up I wonder if I should go in and pray to the Blessed Virgin for dangerous currents.

I wander up to Nigel's but his car is gone and Gilly isn't in the window. The complex is a graveyard. I'm not surprised no one saw the cinderblock crash through my father's door.

The Calvinettis' minivan passes me on the way back. They're unloading when I get home and one of the grandsons is so excited that he forgets who he's talking to and tells me his grandmother got sunstroke and is in the hospital. I say "I'm sorry" and his mother tugs the kid away. His memory returns and he pats his butt and mouths, *Bite me.*

I'm very sure that I will never have children.

I sit on the curb. Smoke. Think about tracking down Azzah and giving her a call, but it's been more than a year and that's too long. Think about the smattering of new friends I could have made, girls who tried to be nice despite the rampant "Meredith has cooties" attitude, if only I'd given them a chance instead of rejecting them before they rejected me. Examine my split ends, my toes, my cuticles. Watch a squirrel run along the fence line.

The day is endless without Andy.

I can't stop waiting so I give in and think about what will happen tomorrow when my mother leaves for work and I'm alone with my father.

"No, Daddy, no."

My stomach churns. I rest my head on my knees. Push through the memories and make my vows.

I won't shower after the assault. I'll call 911 as soon as he's finished.

"Please stop!"

If I'm still coherent I'll tell the counselors and cops every detail and watch them grow huge with anger. I'll talk forever as they swab for samples because now I know that his punishment will spring from the details I provide.

"I don't want to get him in trouble. . . ."

I *do* want to get him in trouble. I should have told all the first time instead of worrying that my mother would hate me. That she wouldn't love me anymore.

Now I know better. She might have loved me once when I was small and cute and a harmonious accessory, but never, never did she love me as much as she wanted him.

"Your father made a mistake, everybody makes mistakes, Meredith! Why did you have to ruin our family?"

I will not take the blame for his perversion. If I can stay sane, I can send him to prison for life or at least until

185

I turn eighteen, which will give me three more years of peace.

I will save other kids from my father and hopefully I will save myself, too.

I lift my head. Wipe my face.

These are my vows.

The rest depends on the nature of the beast.

chapter twenty-three

My parents get home after 10:00, right as I'm washing down the last of tomorrow's vitamins with V8. I pull the band from my hair and shake the curtain closed over my face. "Have a good time?" I ask as they clatter into the kitchen on a salty, fishy breeze.

"Oh, it was great," my mother burbles, slinging her beach bag onto the table and heading straight for the fridge. Her hair is spiky from wind and salt and her eyebrows are pale slashes against her sunburn. "The best I've had in a long time." She laughs and a gust of stale, alcoholic exhale blows through the room.

"Good." The rich smell of broiled coconut oil on my father's skin turns my stomach. "I'm going to bed." I try to sidle past, but he anticipates it and casually blocks my exit.

"Already?" he says, accepting the bottle of spring water my mother hands him. "Why? We just got home." He slings a strong arm around my neck and pulls me against him. "C'mon, you must have missed us just a little."

"Nope." The flames from his body steal my breath and I twist free before they incinerate me. "I had my own stuff to do."

"Oh yeah, like what?" my father says and the teasing drops from his tone. "You know, we never did talk about where you go running off to—"

"Charles, please, not now," my mother interrupts, twining her arms around his waist and smiling up into his face. "We had such a nice day; let's not ruin it." She snuggles closer. "Besides, fifteen-year-olds need their secrets, too, you know."

"Secrets?" he says, shrugging out of her embrace. "Don't be ridiculous. What kind of secrets could a kid have, Sharon?"

She flushes. Doesn't look at me. Smoothes her hair and says with studied nonchalance, "Oh, you know. Normal girl-type stuff. Best friends and diaries and—"

"Do you keep a diary, Chirp?" He sounds intrigued, like he wants to know if he's been the star in my private show, the jock stud of my daydreams.

"No," I say flatly and edge past him out of the kitchen. "Mom, wake me up before you leave for work tomorrow, okay? Good night."

He knocks on my door a half hour later. My mother's in the shower and I'm completing my pyramid alarm on top of the beanbag chair in front of the door.

"Meredith?" he says quietly.

"What?" I say.

"Open the door."

"No," I say loudly. "I'm getting ready to go to bed."

"Shhh. Just for a minute."

"No! What is it? I can hear you fine from here."

The pipes clank as the shower goes off in the bathroom.

"Never mind," he mutters irritably. "I'll talk to you to-morrow. And don't plan on running out of here early. I mean it. You and I have some serious catching up to do."

Yes, we do, and I owe him so much. "Fine," I say and put the finishing touches on my pyramid. Its foundation is unstable and its balance precarious; one nudge will reduce it to rubble.

I shut off the light and peer through the blinds. No patrol car, no Nigel and Gilly. I flatten my cheek against the glass and can just make out the dark corner of Andy's building. I watch for a moment but nothing changes. I climb into bed without undressing, without building my pillow bunker or my window pyramid.

Drunken mobs never rampage on Sunday nights. The attack, when it comes, will be friendly fire.

I lie wide-eyed in the dark, listening. The obscene waits outside my door, counting the minutes until dawn when it will come at me again. And why not? What's going to stop it? Laws, prison, and counseling didn't. The distant threat of eternal damnation pales in comparison to the immediate gratification of corrupting young skin.

I draw a quiet, shaky breath and glance over at the Madonna.

She gazes back, serene and unblinking.

I've been hoping for a save in the last inning but now, when all the outfield chatter has faded and the other players have gone home, the only one stepping up to the plate is me.

chapter twenty-four

Coffee. Toilets flush. Daylight leaks through the blinds. My eyeballs have been rolled in sand. I creak out of bed and kick the beanbag chair. The pyramid collapses.

Voices. "Don't forget the glass man is coming at one."

"Now how could I forget that, Sharon?"

"I'm just trying to help."

"I know but I'm a big boy, okay? I don't need another mother."

"Fine. Forget I ever said anything." Silence. Running water. "I'd forgotten how cranky you were in the morning."

"I just don't like people nagging me the minute I get up."

"I wasn't . . . forget it." Compact snaps closed. "Zip me up, please."

"Okay. Watch your hair."

"Ow."

"I *said* watch your hair. Christ, who wears a turtleneck in the summer, anyway?"

"The store is air-conditioned. What is wrong with you this morning? Are you trying to piss me off or what?"

His silence hones the tension.

"So what are you and Meredith going to do today?"

Sigh. "Nothing. Don't worry about it. Just lay off the third degree, all right, Sharon? Now, do you want a cup of coffee?"

Silence. "Sure. Fine. I'll be out in a minute. Thanks."

Heavy footsteps pass my door. Lighter ones hurry into the bedroom.

I drag the beanbag chair away and cross the hall to the vacated bathroom. Pee, wash my face, and rush back to my room.

My mother knocks softly as I'm strapping on my overalls. "Meredith?"

"I'm up," I say, jamming my feet into work boots. Double-knot the ties. My feet have spread out from going barefoot and now feel trapped and smothered under layers of socks and leather.

"Open up for a minute."

I pack my survival gear into my pockets. Turn on the teddy cam, open the door, and am greeted by a choking cloud of perfume. "What?"

She steps inside. Glances worriedly over her shoulder and says, "Look, I don't know what's eating your father, but he's in a rotten mood so just be nice and don't antagonize him, okay?" A jagged-edged hickey peeks out over the top of her turtleneck. It wasn't there when they came home from the shore last night. "I had to pay for everything yesterday and I think it hit him that I'm the only one earning any money. It's hard on a man to be unemployed. The simplest things make them cranky." She sighs. "So just be good, will you?"

Be good. Be a nice girl. Don't ruin our happy family.

A searing flash cuts a chasm in my surface calm and I shock myself by saying, "Please don't leave me here alone with him, Mom." Whose plaintive voice is this? Not mine. Never mine.

The pain is scalding. "No, Daddy, no," I beg, hysterical. "Mommy! Mommy!"

I want my mother. I have always wanted my mother.

"Oh Meredith, please, not now," she mutters, rubbing her forehead and glancing toward the kitchen. "We have to trust each other if we're ever going to be a real family again, can't you see that? Your father's trying so hard and it hurts him so much when you back away. So please, try just a little. For me." She looks straight into my eyes for the first time in years and somehow it's worse than not being seen at all. "Promise?"

Pain digs deep inside of me. "Fine." The vow is void the moment it falls from my lips.

"Good," she says and smiles. "That's one less thing I

have to worry about." She hurries off to meet my father and I am left in my four-sided box, alone.

So I leave the teddy cam running, follow her into the kitchen, and make the one-word answers she requires of me. I don't know when the basslike rumbling in my brain starts, but every time my father speaks it increases in intensity. Not in volume but in agitation.

My mother kisses my father good-bye and leaves.

The air vibrates.

I sit at the table with my back to the wall, one hand welded to a mug of steaming coffee, the other to the knife in my pocket. I move my thumb and press the smoke alarm camera remote. I would give anything to be someone else.

"Well." My father leans back in his chair, cocks his head, and smiles. "We're finally alone." He waits but I don't answer. "What, now that your mother's gone you have nothing to say? C'mon, Chirp, you used to be such a chatterbox. Fill me in. Give me an update on the last three years."

"They were great," I say.

"That's not what I wanted to hear," he says after a moment.

I say nothing. Acid eats my stomach.

"I was hoping you'd say you missed me like I missed you." His hand creeps across the table like a hairless tarantula until it touches mine. "There's so much I want to say but you make it so hard." He strokes the claws curved around the coffee cup. "Don't punish me, baby. Look at me. I need to see your eyes."

I can't. I won't. If I look, I die.

"C'mon, Chirp." His fingers wander past my hand to my wrist. "Give it up. I'm not such a bad guy. Really. I love you, sweetheart. Just let me love you again."

Leah Louisa, Nigel. Ms. Mues, I need your God. Andy, come home. The rumbling is ferocious. "You're not ever going to stop, are you?" My voice is a thin, flat blade.

The thumb stroking my wrist stills. "Stop what? Loving you? Wanting you? No. Not until the day I die."

So that's it, then. I could put him away again and again, and again and again he'll get out and come for me. It will never, ever end. "Dad, please." I push the words past the lump in my throat. "You don't understand. You have to let me go. *Please.*"

"Chirp," he says softly. "Just stop, all right? It's not gonna change anything."

My head jerks up and for an instant our gazes lock.

I shove away from the table but am still anchored by his grip. Release my coffee mug and watch in slow motion as the cup hits the table and the steaming brew splashes, as he instinctively releases my wrist and jumps back.

"Whoa!" He grabs a place mat and drops it on the spreading spill. "What the hell are you doing? You could have burned us both!" He looks up and catches me backing away. "Oh, no you don't. Get over here and help me clean this up."

I shake my head. He likes it. Look at his eyes gleam. Ready to pounce. How much is enough? My work boots keep retreating. Fight or flight. Sacrifice me. Do it. *Do it.*

"Come on, now," he says, skirting the table and slowly coming toward me. "This is getting out of hand. What're you so jumpy about?" And then he lunges faster than I can wheel and run, and my back is to the wall, my head hits the wall and his arms close around me and the rumbling in my mind drowns his apologies and declarations of love. My head sinks and the golden baseball strung around his neck presses hard and cold against my mouth.

"Oh God, baby, I missed you so much. I don't want to hurt you." His body is burning and his hands are everywhere, gripping, squeezing, rushing to unlatch my overall straps.

I am small and growing smaller. A desperate wail reverberates through my brain and I can feel the memory of blood running rivulets down my legs. "Mommy," I whisper.

His head snaps up and he turns toward the door.

My shove catches him by surprise and knocks him backward.

I bolt for my bedroom.

"Meredith!"

Holy Mary, Mother of God, pray for us sinners now and at the hour of our death. The silent litany flows unbidden. *Queen of families, have mercy. Help me.*

I shoot inside as my father thunders down the hall. Slam the door but he's there, right there, turning the knob as I fight to lock it and he's stronger than me so I back away with my own breathless blubbering in my ears, wordless terror a jagged, stuttering, "Hunh . . . hunh . . . hunh . . ." and the Blessed Virgin watches from my nightstand as he clamps down on my shoulders.

Bared teeth. Absolute intent.

Game over.

Paralysis comes and goes. In a flash I'm berserk, all claws and work boots. "I *hate* you!" I grind out, wild because I'm *not* going to be the one torn and bloody again, raped on camera, the pathetic victim sacrifice absorbing the sick pain of the sick fucking world. I'll kill him first, I will, and somewhere deep inside of me, I realize I've always known it.

He grabs my hair and yanks my head back, exposing my face.

I go still. Adrenaline floods my veins, numbing me for the final blow.

His fingers tighten, bringing tears to my eyes. "Don't ever say that again." He licks his lips. "Now lay down." Releases my hair and shoves me backward onto the bed. Unzips his pants. "Take off those disgusting overalls."

The weight in my pocket nudges my thigh, suddenly becomes my knife. I put my hand to its unforgiving outline and can't stop crying years of tears because if I don't stab my father with my weapon, then he is going to stab me with his.

Palsied and blind, I fumble my hand into my pocket.

"What're you doing?" he says and reaches for my arm. "What is that?"

My fingers close around the knife but I can't get it open. I jerk away from him, panting, squirming backward across the mattress toward the headboard.

He seizes my ankles and drags me back. "What is that?" He kneels on the bed and grabs my flailing arm. "Give it to me."

"No!" I twist and kick, but he pins me down, relentless, pulling me into the abyss and I know I'm losing, cracking, breathing in the impossible scent of roses and dark, rich soil as the golden baseball dances above me, flashing, mocking, and the Madonna stands steadfast and serene, a savior still within reach.

Queen of martyrs. Mirror of justice.

I stop fighting. Flick my wrist and the knife sails toward the door.

"Goddamn you, Chirp, what the hell *is* that?" my father

snaps and releases me. The bed bounces as he backs off and turns to retrieve it.

I wipe my eyes and reach for the Holy Mother. Close my hands around the heavy, solid oak statue and with my own tears anointing my palms, rise up behind my father.

He straightens.

I plant my feet in a batter's stance and swing.

chapter twenty-five

I sit on the front steps. My stomach heaves and I just manage to part my knees before I vomit on the step below. Wipe my mouth on my arm and realize I'm shaking.

I think I'm in shock. The sun is brutal and I should be sweating, but my skin is cool and clammy. I gaze up the road to the bend. The world is tilted and the scenery jumbled, sharp-edged and carnival bright.

Nigel rounds the bend in a shuffling run, shouting into his cellphone.

I don't remember calling him, but I must have, because a squad car screams into sight, passing him and squealing up to my curb.

I grope for the railing. Stand. Wobble down past the splattered vomit. "Virgin most powerful," I croak and one of the cops says, "What?" like he didn't hear me, but it's too late because the world spins crazy and I'm gone.

chapter twenty-six

My mother is arrested and charged with a list of offenses, including leaving me alone with a known pedophile. The judge grants bail because she is not considered a flight risk.

She hasn't contacted me. Not even a note.

She spends her days at the hospital with my father. She doesn't understand it yet, but he is my gift to her. He is all hers now; she wins by default as there is no one else in the race. Well, except for the newly fertilized egg she's carrying, but she's got a couple of months yet to decide whether or not she really wants to share him again with someone else.

My guess is no.

The doctors reviewed the nanny cam tapes and agreed that although the blunt-force trauma from the oaken icon was sure to do *some* damage, it should not have been enough to cause my father a C4 spinal-cord injury resulting in quadriplegia.

But somehow it was.

The doctors say my father has some function below the level of the injury. He can move his head and neck and has limited shoulder movement. The rest of him is paralyzed, but with technological advances and assistance devices like a chin controller and voice recognition, he can still go online or operate an electric wheelchair.

He is also under arrest. Big time.

Nigel relays the news. His voice is grave, but his eyes glow with triumph.

It's been four days now, but it's still hard to believe I'm done being hunted.

I hold one quiet, curious card close to my vest and only play it with Nigel, even though he's a bigger skeptic than I am. Was. Am.

"But don't you think it's weird that Andy left the Madonna in case I needed her and she's what saved me? I mean, I know that's not how he meant it and all, but still," I say on Friday as we amble down Leah Louisa's quiet, tree-lined street. She's my official guardian now and the rose room my new home. I stick my hands into my empty shorts pockets. The police have confiscated my knife and Leah Louisa, my cigarettes.

The Dumpster got my overalls.

"Hell no. *You're* what saved you, kid. Not divine intervention." Nigel wedges a cigarette in his mouth and offers me one.

I look around and accept. No doubt word will somehow get back to my grandmother and she'll insist we discuss my addiction with my new therapist, but I don't mind. It'll be good to argue about something normal for a change.

He lights them and squints at me through the smoke. "You know what? Check that. You know better than I do what happened and if thinking you had a little help along the way worked for you, then who am I to say it didn't?" He shrugs. "Point being, I got no solid answer on this one. You need to decide for yourself."

"I know," I say and linger in the shade of a massive maple tree. I run my fingers along its craggy bark. It's weathered what, a hundred seasons and still it stands fast, roots deep and branches spreading. "So you honestly think it was just a coincidence?"

He sighs and hitches up his saggy jeans. "Does it really matter what I think?"

"Yes," I say and meet his gaze. "It always has. You're the best man I know."

He looks away. Blinks and rubs his eyes. "Damn smoke." Catches me in a brief, one-armed embrace that's more headlock than hug. "All right, honestly, between you and me? I think you got the rest of your life to figure it out."

"Gee, thanks," I whisper and snort a laugh into his rumpled sport shirt.

"Don't mention it." His cellphone rings and he releases me. Digs it from his pocket and answers. "Balthazar. Hey, how're you doing?" His considering gaze searches my face. "Yeah, she's right here. No, I didn't. Sure. In about ten minutes. Hold on." He hands me the phone. "It's Andy." He turns and ambles a few yards down the block to give me some privacy.

"Andy?" I say into the phone, breathless.

"Mer? Are you okay?"

"I'm fine. I made it, Andy. It's done." Hearing his voice has me near tears and suddenly I can't wait to be with him, to be *new* with him, and to tell him yes, he was right, all things are possible and there actually may be such things as miracles. "Where are you? Are you still on your way home? Did Nigel tell you what happened?"

"We're home, Mer. We never got there."

"What?" I stare at Nigel's broad back. "I . . . why not?"

"The guy died," Andy says simply. "The victim soul, I mean."

"Oh my God," I say, straightening. "That's awful. What happened?"

"Huh?" he says, distracted. "Oh, uh, wait a minute. Okay. Sorry. Uh, we got to the motel Sunday night and my mother called to confirm our meeting for Monday. His wife said he was really agitated and told us to call back the next morning to make sure he was up to having visitors. We called Monday morning before we got back on the road, and they said he'd passed away maybe a half hour earlier."

"So you never even got to see him," I say, leaning against a tree. "That sucks."

Andy sighs. "I guess. The brochure said he'd been a victim soul for like sixty years, bedridden, in and out of a coma. He'd received more than three thousand of the faithful over his lifetime and that's a lot of human suffering for one person to absorb. Too much, maybe. Now I'm kind of glad I didn't add to it."

He sounds different, subdued but not devastated, and it leaves me at a loss. "Oh. Well, that's good, I guess." Is it? I don't know. This conversation isn't anything like I thought it would be. I thought he'd say he loved me, that he'd be dying to know what had happened between me and my father, and how soon could I get there to see him, but so far, nothing. A low-level dread settles over me. "So, when did you get home?"

A heartbeat hesitation. "Tuesday morning," he says, and the words echo like a death knell in the ensuing silence. "I know I should have called sooner, but I talked to Nigel and you had so much going on and I didn't want to . . . what?" He says impatiently, off to the side. "Hold on, Mer." He covers the phone but I can still hear him. "I *am*, Mom. Give me a chance." Uncovers the phone. "Listen, it's too much to go into right now. I'll tell you the next time I see you, okay?"

"I . . . okay." So this is it then. The moment I've feared since we first met. Funny, how I'd prepared for his leaving me if he could walk and I'd prepared for his leaving me because of my father being around, but what I'd never prepared for was his leaving me while still paralyzed and with my father safely gone. "But you know I'm not living there anymore, right? I'm at Leah Louisa's now. I can't just cut out of here and come over." I wait, barely breathing, sinking into the gaping silence. "Hello?"

"Yeah, I know," he says and sounds distracted. "Everything's different now. Look, I've got to go. Are you going to be there for a while? Good. Give me your grandmother's number and I'll call you back in like half an hour, okay?"

Will you? I think dully, but give him the number anyway. He says good-bye and hangs up, leaving me standing with the dead phone pressed to my ear like an empty seashell.

"You okay, kid?" Nigel says and eases the phone from my hand.

I blink at him, mute.

He fidgets. Checks his watch. "I was gonna tell you that they never made it to Iowa. They turned around and came home." He pulls a crumpled hanky from his pocket and mops his florid face. "Come on, let's head back to your granny's house. This heat is rough on a fat old man."

Numb, I fall into step beside him. "You told them what happened?"

"Yeah, and I should have known better than to talk religion with Paula," Nigel says, shaking his head and plodding on every crack in the sidewalk. "Jesus, she's excitable. As soon as I told her you whacked your old man with the statue Monday morning she ripped off those ugly glasses and went down on her knees in some kind of swoon—"

He's talking too much, clobbering the silence so I won't say anything, won't burst into tears and buckle under the weight of this last, awful straw.

And I won't. Not yet, anyway.

He stops in front of my grandmother's house and checks his watch again. "Well, I guess I'm gonna get going. Gilly needs walking and I've got a sh— er, crapload of errands to run. Did I tell you Paula's car broke down at the entrance to the complex, right in front of the Cambridge Oaks sign?" The ghost of his old, easy grin breaks through. "It took the towing company half a day to get out and move it and the association was having hissy fits. I've got to hand it to Paula, though; she let 'em sweat a while before she told 'em she was finally junking it. Now I'm her ride till she gets another car." His smile fades and he flushes, uncomfortable, like now that I'm not in the condo loop anymore we

209

have nothing in common. "Let me go. I'll get headquarters to release the Madonna statue out of Evidence and bring it back to you as soon as I can."

I shake my head. "No, it's Andy's. Give it to him." I tuck back my hair and look him straight in the eye. He needs to know that I know it's all over. "You'll see him again before I will."

His mouth opens and closes. "Yeah. Okay." He hesitates and in an odd gesture, chucks me gently under the chin. "Keep the faith, kid," he says and lumbers off to his car.

I watch him drive away, wanting nothing more than to sit on the curb and bawl, but the people on this street don't huddle with their feet in the gutter so I wander into the house, past Leah Louisa unloading the dishwasher, and end up in the den. I flop down onto the couch and wonder what just happened. Somehow four splintered into three and one, and I never even saw it coming.

"Did you have a nice talk with Nigel?" Leah Louisa calls from the kitchen.

"Yeah, pretty much," I say, staring at the ceiling. It's smooth, off-white, a big blank canvas with no tiles to count and no memories staining the surface.

It's just a ceiling.

I close my eyes and think of Andy, who prayed so hard and got so little, and of the Madonna, whose presence saved me from a fate worse than death and at the same time somehow sentenced my father to the exact same thing.

Think even harder for a minute, then get up and go straight to the bookcase.

There's a question I need answered.

Mystical Rose. Virgin most powerful.

I slip out the sliding glass door and settle on the stone wall outlining the patio. The sweet, cotton-candy scent of a hundred blooming irises rides the breeze.

Mother most merciful. Cause of our joy.

I think of grander plans and coincidence, of the victim soul's death and my father's inexplicable paralysis. I think of how amazing it is that I'm not a murderer.

A victim soul is a pious individual chosen to absorb the pain and suffering of others.

My father isn't pious. He attends no services and worships no god.

Unless there's something I've missed.

I open the dictionary and page to the Ps. Run my finger down the column until I find it.

"Pious."

There are several definitions. I didn't know that.

"Showing reverence for deity and devotion to divine worship." No. "Marked by conspicuous religiosity." No. "Marked by sham or hypocrisy." Oh. I stop, heart pound-

211

ing. Read it again. " 'Marked by sham or hypocrisy.' "
Slowly lift my head. "*Now* I get it."

Mother inviolate. Mirror of justice.

"Meredith?" Leah Louisa stands at the sliding glass door. "Nigel and Paula Mues are here, and they brought along a young man named Andy who wants very much to see you." She steps aside to let him through.

I tuck my hair back behind my ears.

Meet his shining gaze and break into a smile.

He is so tall.

such a pretty girl
by laura wiess
READING GROUP GUIDE

DISCUSSION QUESTIONS

1. Meredith frequently refers to numbers throughout the novel—how many tiles there are in the bathroom, the amount of multivitamins she takes, and four being her "safety number." Why does Meredith find such comfort in numbers?

2. Discuss the theme of paralysis in *Such a Pretty Girl* and how it applies to each character.

3. "Ms. Mues shields me just to thwart my father. She doesn't really care for me. She's a plotter, a planner and what better way to avenge her son than to destroy her enemy's daughter? To gain my trust and use me to achieve her goal, much like my father used Andy . . ." (page 73). Do you think this is true? What is Ms. Mues's motivation for moving into Meredith's neighborhood?

4. "Four is my best number, but there are four years between my parents too, and I would rather fall down dead than find out we're anything like them" (page 74). How is the relationship between Andy and Meredith different than the relationship between Meredith's parents? Do you think Meredith is repeating her mother's mistake?

5. "A victim soul is a pious individual chosen to absorb the suffering of others" (page 86). Who do you think acts as the victim soul in this novel? Does this person accept his/her role willingly?

6. "Andy's demons chase him just as hard as yours chase you" (page 114). How are Andy and Meredith different in dealing with their mutual psychological scars?

7. What is the significance of each of the recurring images in the novel: the Dumpster, the gold baseball pendant, roses, and the statue of Mary.

8. Discuss the relationship between Sharon and Charles. Why does she stay with him despite everything he's done? Meredith believes her mother will always choose her husband over her daughter. Is this true? If so, why does she want Meredith to stay with them instead of with her grandmother?

9. "It's the stuff that no one sees that does the most damage" (page 10). Sight is another theme in *Such a Pretty Girl*. What does each character choose not to see and how does that hurt them?

10. What do you think Meredith's future will be like? Will she become the stereotype of abused children? Or will she become its exception?

AUTHOR QUESTIONS

1. Other than to expose an unthinkable crime, what motivated you to write Meredith's story?

Meredith did. I know that sounds odd, but she came to me as a real girl, stuck in the middle of a real hell, and I couldn't turn away.

2. What kind of child molestation cases did you research while writing this book? Did you base any parts of *Such a Pretty Girl* on real cases?

All kinds of cases, unfortunately. There's plenty of information out there: first person accounts, prison statistics, injury reports, sexual offender crimes and classifications, documentaries like the unforgettable *Just Melvin; Just Evil* directed by James Ronald Whitney, and professional opinions on sexual predator recidivism rates after release from prison. I processed a lot of raw, detailed information, including revisiting the memory of the disgusting grope *I* got when I was twelve, from one of my girlfriends' fathers. Up until that moment, I'd never even imagined anyone's father would ever do something like that. It was quite a rude awakening. Meredith's story wasn't based on any one case, but grew right from the characters themselves.

3. This novel can be read easily in one sitting and the story takes places within a few days. Was the writing process fluid? Or did you work on it for a long time?

Pretty Girl's first draft was written in a white-hot blast of terror, fury and despair. Once Meredith started talking, once I knew what was going on, there was no stopping. I was with her all the way, and let me tell you; most times it wasn't such a good place to be. Once the first draft was complete, I had to back off and let it cool down, so I could look at it again with a more dispassionate eye. The book evolved, as it needed to, over the course of several years.

4. How did the idea of a victim soul become such a prevalent part of the story?

Somewhere in my brain, random bits of information separate from all the other daily stuff, weave themselves together without any conscious effort on my part, and one day, pretty much out of the blue, just *present* themselves. It's very cool. I remember hearing of the supposed phenomenon of victim souls years ago, and the idea both fascinated and repelled me. I was wandering around online and found a website for one of the current victim souls, complete with photos. It blew my mind to imagine life the way this person was living, but that was it, and I went on about my business. Later, when *Pretty Girl* was born, it all swept back and somehow fell into place.

5. How would you like to see the laws regarding child molesters change?

This is a dangerous question to ask someone who's spent so much time researching, imagining and absorbing, in vivid detail, the agony, terror, and misery of children who have been victimized at the hands of adults. I'd like to see the punishment finally fit the severity of the crime. For example, raping a minor, age infant through five, at the very *least* earns you life with no possibility of parole. Age six to ten buys, say, fifty years, no parole, and so on. That may sound harsh, but if you compare it to the crime, then is it too harsh a sentence, or not harsh enough? Talk to the police, or any other first responder. Talk to the medical staff who are trying not to break down and be sick at the sight of such a little one, so damaged. This is not a smooth, physically easy crime to commit; this is a brutal, willful act, deliberately ignoring a kid's struggling, crying, screaming, and blood. And some pedophiles do it again, and again, and again.

Add mandatory counseling to the sentence, but don't negotiate time. Don't sell out the victims in some warped, legal barter based more on economics than on the severity of the crime. These kids need to know they can answer the door in a couple of years, and not see their molester standing there smiling and holding an embossed invitation to the party.

6. Are any of the secondary characters—Andy, Nigel, Ms. Mues—based on real people?

Not really, although I've probably been gathering personality traits from all sorts of different places for years, and storing them up in some mental warehouse for future use. For instance, I used to know people who kept a framed, color snapshot of a dead pope in his coffin, in their kitchen. That family was my introduction to the seriously devout, and the memory may have helped in creating Ms. Mues, although she ended up nothing like the people I'd known.

7. Did you worry that including a religious element in your book would turn some readers off?

No. It's been my experience that most readers are open-minded enough to entertain almost any element in the course of a story, as long as it's true to the character that lives it. It doesn't mean *you* have to believe it, it just means you're willing to go along for a while with the character that does. No big deal.

READER TIPS

1. Visit Laura Wiess's blog at *http://gypsyrobin.livejournal.com*.

2. Did this book inspire you to get involved in protecting your community? Go to *www.fbi.gov/hq/cid/cac/states.htm* to find information on sex offenders who might be living in your neighborhood.

3. Watch the documentary highly recommended by the author, *Just Melvin: Just Evil*.